Evergreen

Evergreen

an anthology

Edited by Debz Hobbs-Wyatt and Gill James

For Mandy
Happy Christmas
2022

love from

[signature]

see
p. 180

Bridge House

British Library Cataloguing in Publication Data

A Record of this Publication is available from the British
Library

ISBN 978-1-914199-36-3

This edition published 2022 by Bridge House Publishing
Manchester, England

Contents

Introduction

For this year's anthology we asked writers to consider the theme "evergreen". Naturally that makes us think of the Christmas tree. There are indeed some stories that feature that wonderful entity. They all include a deeper understanding of what it means to be evergreen or even ever green.

We choose the stories anonymously. As we select, we have no idea who has written what. It's always exciting putting the names to the texts.

All of what we read was of publishable quality so it was very difficult to have to reject some stories. Therefore if your story hasn't been selected, don't be disheartened.

Again we are pleased to welcome several writers we have published previously and as well as some newcomers to our imprint.

Some of the stories have a Christmas theme, others tell about what is lasting and some deal with nature. Everything green is very important to all of us right now.

It is always a privilege to work with such talented writers.

We hope you will enjoy this year's selection.

Adonis Against the Odds

Dianne Stadhams

I never set out to court Trouble. Quite the opposite, I just try to blend in and meander through life with minimum aggravation. Despite my philosophy, Trouble loves to lurk and clearly rejoices in its reveal… often at my expense.

When I was a kid and the bullies came out to play, literally WITH me you understand, good old Trouble could be relied upon to be there in the mix. Instead of a football, use Adonis. He rolls well. Ha, ha.

Secondary school was the usual nightmare of too much testosterone, bragging about sexual exploits that were only ever fantasies, posing to attract female attention in a way that was supposed not to look obvious… but was totally so and desperately pathetic. In my case it was a joke to try to be anything other than the class clown… whether I wanted the role or not… which I didn't. But why invoke Trouble with a rejection?

At university I came into my own. Women loved me. I was more pet than predator, safe company, someone to confide in about the woes of romance and romping. Want a great lover? My free advice is to not choose the tall, dark handsome that captures the gaze of all who enter his orbit. Look for the pigeon not the peacock. Check out the quiet one who sidles around the outer rim of those who boast… and will be fickle. If you don't have to try hard then you don't value what you seduce. I was the one who learnt to look, listen and learn… with the ladies. Or ladettes as ladies would not be an accurate description of the females I hung around with.

"Oh Adonis, your heart is your soul," the girls would sigh.

That's me. Adonis the connoisseur of the ways of XX chromosomes.

I might not have been the Romeo of their dreams but when I had my way my lovers were guaranteed satisfaction and discretion. An un-iced cupcake still tastes sweet.

For this story to make sense there are six things about me I'd like to share.

Firstly, there's my name. What do you reckon – parents with a sense of humour or a statement of intent? You choose after you've read who I am.

Secondly, I climb Everest regularly. No, not that one... a sixteen hands horse... that's a big animal if you aren't in the know about nags... named after the Himalayan peak. Everest was a birthday present. The original suggestion had been a cute Shetland pony, named Colin.

Really?

Nothing wrong with the beast but riding Colin was not the image I intended to project. In Gaelic, Colin means young pup. No way was this Adonis teaming up with a short-arsed horse. My Everest was a brute with a big heart. Too big, the vet confirmed as she diagnosed a congenital heart murmur. The advice was that the horse should not be ridden hard or long or by anyone overweight. Me and Everest bonded immediately. I winked at him. He whinnied in response and I knew... no Trouble. Horse and man had been dismissed as rejects. Everest and I were made for each other.

Thirdly, I can toss a caber... that's a six-metre, larch pole weighing seventy-nine kilos, the sport of note in the Scottish Highland Games. It might look comical... obscene even... which made victory all the more pleasurable... with no Trouble anticipated. My opponents often gawped in disbelief when I stood ready to throw my pole. More fool them for losing concentration or underestimating the ratio of pole length to personal height. Aren't there stories about David and Goliath, Jack and the Giant up the beanstalk? There is definitely great satisfaction in outwitting Trouble's plans.

Fourthly, I'm a doctor. Not of the blood and guts kind, although I've seen enough of that when Trouble hangs around. The vicious football role in my youth can attest to that. I became adept at bandaging wounds and applying ointments... to myself. I have a PhD in the history of rhododendrons. Very esoteric... I can hear you wince. But someone's got be an expert in the field of woody plants. And when it comes to rhododendrons I'm a mastermind. Did you know they symbolise danger? No, most people don't. I've never sat next to anyone at a dinner party who had a clue. Once, a fellow diner, after a glass or three, asked if it would have been more in tune for me to study azaleas, which technically speaking are a subgenus of rhododendron. Caustic or what? I don't do small.

"You can be a tall person but small minded," I replied. The person changed the subject.

Fifthly, I get labelled a dwarf, one of the little people below 147 centimetres in height. That's possibly the least interesting thing about me, which is why I left it towards the end of my list to share.

If you want to ask why would I aim to acquire such a disparate set of skills the answer is simple. BECAUSE, that's why... JUST BECAUSE. No explanation will be forthcoming. Were you caught off guard? Don't fret. Outsiders and freaks can have that effect.

That brings me to the sixth thing of significance. How does a caber-tossing, horse-riding, academic dwarf end up bedding the beauty queen of one of the most famous flower festivals in the world? In summary... mishap invite...

mixed messages. I thought I was going to be a guest speaker at the festival. I had assembled a PowerPoint presentation illustrated with a hundred images of rhododendron. Alas, the festival believed they had contracted a dwarf to jump naked out of the ten-tier, floral, festival cake and land on a blanket of petals to launch the fireworks spectacular.

All I can say is… there was going to be Trouble with or without the crackers. And Trouble and I, for once, were on the same side.

The big mix up had to be resolved to everyone's satisfaction. One well-intentioned but bum-humoured suggestion by a group of local vintners and brewers was to amend the situation to a dwarf-tossing competition. As a further concession, I, the dwarf, could be clothed. They felt sure that would still guarantee a large number of spectators. One of the group referenced such an event in New Zealand some years previously which had made international headlines and a large amount of money, although it was not clear if any dwarves ended up rich.

However the idea was quashed after a local official pointed out that such an activity was illegal. Quite why the organisers thought I would be happy to be tossed in trousers rather than jump au naturel was not explained.

The festival beauty queen intervened in a rage. Political correctness was one thing. Human rights abuse was quite another. She threatened media exposure and her resignation on the spot.

Trouble over.

I told them I would forget the insult, and not start legal proceedings as long as my fee and conditions for attending the event were met. Then the beauty queen told me her name was Azalea. The name symbolises love and gentleness. What were the chances? Fate trumped Trouble… it was written in the flowers!

I retired to my luxury hotel suite and ordered everything expensive listed on the room service menu (the perk of an appeasement condition). My beauty queen joined me slipping into something comfortable that was more conducive to oysters and champagne. To be precise, Azalea dropped her prickly, stiff tulle, crinoline, rose bud costume on the floor.

"Life is short," she said.

"So am I."

It would have been churlish not to mirror her style and accommodate her approach.

"Well, I never," said Azalea studying my naked body with its perfectly-proportioned genitalia that might make any lothario envious.

"You have now," I replied whilst pouring the bubbles and toasting to our auspicious rendezvous.

We spent the weekend proving that a small man can be a giant lover.

Six months later we moved into together.

Ten years on I named my hybrid rhododendron in her honour. It has won awards in all six countries to which it's been exported.

Our eight-year-old daughter, who is already 128 centimetres, prefers to watch synchronised swimming in a heated pool to men tossing cabers outdoors amongst the midges. She has a Shetland pony named No Trouble (guess whose suggestion?) that is shorter than us both. The photograph in the local paper of her collecting her first gymkhana rosette flanked by proud parents has a caption which reads:

NO TROUBLE with ADONIS and his AZALEAS.

Reader, against the odds I have blossomed into an evergreen with accolades... whose size is measured in love!

About the author

Dianne Stadhams is an Australian, resident in the UK, who works globally in marketing and project management. With a PhD in visual anthropology she has used creative tools – drama, dance, radio, video – to empower others in some of the world's poorest nations. She believes passionately that the arts are valuable tools to promote social cohesion, provoke debate and influence attitudes, mind sets and actions.

www.stadhams.com

All her Tomorrows

Chris Simpson

The last time Tom had seen Sandra was just before the attack. He'd never know if that was why she left him, but he almost came to accept it as the reason.

Since leaving, her mobile no longer received his calls. No letters came. Nor did he receive any message, for months, of where she had gone or if she was okay.

As good as dead, he believed that she must still be out there doing nothing more than living and refusing to send him even a postcard.

He didn't feel good about the attack. Never would. But what really smarted was when he wondered how a person could hurt another the way she had.

It was a Saturday.

He'd been at work in the morning, installing two air conditioners. The caretaker, a balding chatty type who had nothing better to do that day than open up the school and tell Tom about his life, which he laughingly said involved staying away from his wife as much as possible, kept plying him with coffee. Tom's fifty-year-old bladder tried in vain to contain the contents of cup after cup. When the battle was lost, Tom demounted the scaffold tower, which creaked and rattled alarmingly. But Tom couldn't say no to the caretaker when offered yet another cup. As he sipped and smiled at the man who would not stop talking, Tom wished he could've at least said no to the job and had gone to see Orient, or gone down the pub, or had just stayed on the sofa watching TV before having to go out that evening.

Once home, after being stuck in London's never-ending

traffic, despite the day and time, Tom shaved. Rushing, he cut himself on the chin, leaving a mark.

While waiting for a taxi, he smoked on the doorstep. Taking a break from pondering at the dark blue sky, he turned behind him to see Sandra applying lipstick, concentrating into the hallway mirror. He used to say she looked good but some argument, long ago and forgotten to the point where only the result remained, meant he couldn't do it today; he was as good as a child frozen on a high diving board.

At Chingford Station, they met up with Caroline and Eric. Tom wondered why they, and his wife, were all dressed up. The show was just a musical about Motown, not a wedding or Royal Ascot which they went to religiously.

As they walked, Tom nodded to Eric. "What you wearing that for?"

"Got to make an effort."

"You look like you're going to court."

"Fuck me, Tom. We can't all pull off your look."

Tom put his hands in his pockets. "What look would that be?"

"As if you're traipsing round Benidorm."

"I like Benidorm," Tom said, part in joke, part in truth.

On the train back home, Tom wasn't happy to let the evening end. The musical had been as he thought – predictable. He couldn't see the point in going, knowing he would have had more fun with a tenner in a pub jukebox.

Sitting next to Eric, across from their wives, he leaned towards his friend and whispered, "Reckon we can get a quick pint before we part?"

"You didn't have enough up West?"

"What's tomorrow?" Tom asked.

"Sunday, you daft prick."

"Exactly."

Eric laughed. "Long day, son?"

"It's been a long life. I fancy one before tucking in."

"Fair do. Let's get a jar."

Outside The Station House, whose population of drinkers was thirty years young than Tom, he was still trying to convince Sandra on having a nightcap.

"Come on, it's just the one."

"You said that after we left the show and we ended up having *two* more," she said and laughed.

Tom knew that laugh. It was a laugh that spoke the unspoken sentence: "And now let's go home." Tom stubbed out his cigarette. "Do you know the good thing about this one, though?"

Sandra planted a smile Tom had seen many times before. "What's that?"

"This one *will* be the final one."

After Tom had bought a second round, insisting on a shot for everyone, which Caroline and Sandra said no to, leading him to drink theirs, he examined the crowd on the small dance floor. He couldn't place the music. It sounded to him of a piano hurtling down some stairs. The dancers seemed to enjoy it.

As he got older the women he focussed his attention on were of his own age. He was unlike his friends who pointed out younger women as they sat in pub gardens. Here though, in the small bar, he stared at the women who would have been the age of his own daughter if he and Sandra had a family – something which he realised, in time, he was relieved for not having. The women's legs, which were the same size as his wife's, had a smoothness he had not seen in years. Staring, he imagined what it would be like to touch them.

Everyone on the dance floor smiled, bar a couple of boys who tried to look mean. He wanted to tell the boys it wasn't worth it. Soon enough they'd be humping tools around, doing jobs they never thought they'd do, for not enough money.

Tom nudged Eric who placed his ear to Tom's mouth. "Just let them see what tomorrow brings, mate. They won't be smiling then!"

Tom laughed as Eric shook his head.

Tom then clapped his hands twice before marching onto the dance floor, shouting to the dancers, although they never heard him, "You hum it, son, I'll play it!"

Despite brushing his teeth and gargling mouthwash, he could still taste strawberries from the shots Sandra and Caroline had passed on.

Downstairs, even after drinking tea, the taste lingered. Sandra's words, spoken as she sat opposite him, also lingered. With them he wanted another shot, several more, and a barrel of beer too. For a brief moment, his nose twitched at the memory of doing coke during his early days as a hod carrier.

Knowing his heart, which kept its beat regular thanks to a pacemaker, he wouldn't be taking cocaine any day soon. He raised his hand. Sandra stopped speaking words he wasn't listening to. "Have we got any Tia Maria?"

Sandra's eyes narrowed. "Why do you want that?"

"I remember last Christmas getting pissed on it and falling asleep before the Queen started up."

"And that's what you want to do now? Get drunk while I tell you I'm leaving you?"

"Can't think of a better time."

"Tom… we're not too old where we can't try something new."

17

"New?"

"Yes, Tom."

"*New*, is it?" Something in the word reminded Tom of what Sandra had said, just before he'd switched off. "How old did you say he was?"

"That doesn't matter."

"What'd you mean? Course it does. If I was in my twenties, with everything ahead of me, I'd fuck anything that moved too – even some old woman well past it."

Sandra sighed. "If you were *you* in your twenties, Tom, I wouldn't be leaving."

Tom swallowed before speaking. "Who the fuck *are* you?" he shouted, pointing at Sandra. "Who are you to walk out on our marriage? I don't recognise you. What can this *boy* give you that I can't?"

Tom picked up his cup and threw it at the wall behind Sandra. As he stood up, she made herself small in her armchair. Fearing he'd do something he'd regret, he walked to the double-doors of the conservatory and punched in every pane of glass; each pane smashing a face of those boys he'd seen earlier on the dance floor: in their twenties with everything for the taking.

Tom didn't know how long it took to destroy the doors. He only came back to himself once he was on the floor, crying into his bloodied hands while Sandra sat behind him rubbing his back; a gesture a mother would give to a child after they'd woken from a nightmare.

Tom smoked in the armchair – the same chair where Sandra had delivered closing time on their marriage. He curled himself into it, like sand resting in the drum of a cement mixer someone had forgot to turn on. Eric sat opposite. He'd made them coffee, which Tom wasn't drinking. As one cigarette came to an end, Tom lit another.

18

Eric examined the conservatory doors. "When you going to get those fixed?"

"Soon, perhaps."

"Oh that's good because it's only been six months."

Tom took a deep drag and blew out smoke when he spoke. "It's all part of a grand makeover."

"That so?"

"That's so."

"And what would you call this look?"

Tom shrugged. "Pissed-off-arsehole-on-a-bender chic?"

"You reckon that's going to sweep the nation?"

"I don't know what people like nowadays."

Eric sat forward. "Mate, you know she ain't coming back."

Tom tapped his cigarette, the ash settling into an empty tin foil case which had once held a Bakewell tart. "Yeah. I know."

"You can't keep this up: only leaving the house for work, me coming over twice a week to check you're alive, seeing you in a bathrobe which looks as old as Moses, stubble on your face and post in the hallway which I keep tripping over. Let's be honest, mate, no one's going to fuck you in this state."

Tom and Eric's eyes met. Their stare lasted long. The ash of Tom's cigarette falling off, his cigarette kept burning until it died at the butt. And then, then Tom laughed.

He kept laughing. Eric joined in.

The two men laughed until their eyes were wet and their coffees cold.

He couldn't do that Saturday as Orient were playing. So, to squeeze in the job, Tom did the yearly annual servicing of the two air conditioners on a Friday evening.

When the chatty caretaker, who was also recently

divorced, realised it was Tom, he said staying behind was a pleasure.

Even though Tom refused the coffee offered, multiple times, the caretaker kept talking as Tom erected the tower and then worked from the platform.

As he opened up the air conditioning unit and tightened a loose connection, he thought about Sandra. It wasn't the first time he'd thought of her that day, nor, he knew, would it be the last before he went to bed, alone. His current thought was better than the ones he'd most commonly had over the previous year; becoming sharper with detail, clearer in its desire to be true. While the caretaker chatted on, Tom daydreamed.

Sandra was reading in a cafe near Kilburn, where she now lived with a man half her age.

He was an actor and while Tom knew his name, had seen his photo online and even watched a couple of clips of him performing, he still couldn't bring himself to say his name (even in the confines of his head). But he could grant himself some peace in his fantasy that the new couple were happy.

In this fantasy, as Sandra read, oblivious to her surroundings, her new man watched her from outside. A dumb little smile came to the actor's face at seeing how lovely Sandra was, how special she was and how good it was that she was in his life.

When Sandra looked up, she was no longer coy or lost or forgotten or talked about or abandoned or slandered. She beamed back at him.

The brown of the actor's eyes was the soil of her new home and Sandra was happy.

In her happiness, Sandra laughed; a laugh which was the joy of her tomorrows and the unmooring from her yesterdays.

About the author

Chris Simpson grew up in Bracknell and Slough. He has worked as a waiter, a cinema projectionist, a shoe salesman, an attendant in an amusement arcade, hiring out construction and demolition tools, a pasty seller, a caretaker for a primary school, a teaching assistant and a tutor. He was a collaborator on a sketch show and has performed as a stand-up comedian.

In 2021 he was published alongside Kit de Waal, Kerry Hudson, Philip Ridley and twenty-five other writers in MainStream from Inkandescent Publishers.

In 2020 he had a special mention for the Spread The Word 2020 Life Writing Prize.

In 2019 he was nominated for the inaugural Agora and PFD Lost The Plot Prize.

In 2018 he was an awardee of the inaugural Spread The Word's London Writers Award.

He received a First in Creative Writing at BA level from Birkbeck University.

In 2016 he was nominated for the Royal Academy and Pin Drop Short Story Award 2016.

He lives in London with his wife. They are broke, but happy. He writes both literary and crime fiction which can be found at: www.writerchrissimpson.com

Anecdote for the Pine Mother

Enna Horn

Woman-Walks-Ahead takes Black-Wolf-Stalking on a walk this morning. Crisp morning, clear winter's morning, scattering light-beams across the jagged pavement of the back roads as the sunrise crests over the neighbouring hilltops. Boots *thunk, thunk, thunk* against the charcoal asphalt, little pebbles scattering beneath the soles. *Pitter-patter, pitter-patter* are the echoes of Black-Wolf-Stalking as he heads towards the right-hand side, walking along the place where a white line should be painted. An immediate drop from the roadside results in a small waterway, erosion and run-off from the recent blizzard melting into a small but perilous river. She glances down at the turned-up cuffs of her jeans, the tan of her boots, the leaf upturned like a hand begging for alms – brown palm, edible alms, floating down the little river.

The world surrounding them locked itself down. In this locking down, she procures her thoughts and drizzles them around her person, gathering birds for the seed, seeds for the harvest. Thoughts tumbling over one another, as foxes do during the penultimate springtime evenings. What will be had for breakfast when they return? Eggs and bacon, ham cut and rolled into fry breads, eggs boiled on the stovetop, eggs. It's slim pickings. Trouble stutters within her breast, a second heartbeat. They have never hungered, but there is a first time for everything. What of the Mother? The Mother beneath their feet, angered and trembling and experiencing birthing pains. What happens when the Mother has nothing else to bear from her womb? When soil and tree grow too ancient, can healing turn to poison?

Perhaps so. But it will not be on this crisp winter's morning. Still, the Mother wishes to heal. Corn Mother, sprouting through the soil each summer. Pine Mother, bursting with cones that clatter onto the ground as Woman-Walks-Ahead paces forward – and then, she pauses.

Sickness has invaded the household. Pine Mother will help with this. She has before.

Pine Mother resides on the left-hand side of the road upon which Woman-Walks-Ahead travels alongside Black-Wolf-Stalking. Six tremendous evergreens, planted in a domino stack, towering, bending but never breaking in the strong winds, regardless of season. She rests within the heart of the third tree: a woman-shape carved by time's passing, her hands held against her heart. And from the silhouette of that heart, sap, slow to drip, candle wax down the white body of a light. For a moment, it reminds Woman-Walks-Ahead of Woman-Who-Came-Before.

Woman-Who-Came-Before lights candles in the midst of blizzards when the power flickers off, when circumstances force the household to remember their ancestors 'methods of living. Firelight sparking from behind the glass door of the iron stove, pot-bellied, roaring and stretching as a lion from the den. All rooms dark, but the dark is not a curse, not always. The dark can be safe, holy. Just as the dark green of the needles gathers on the ground, shed like hair, shed like corn tassels, can be healing.

Woman-Walks-Ahead returns to the present moment. She breathes in. Bitter-scent, sharp and clean. Woman-Who-Came-Before suffers from an unknown illness. Woman-Walks-Ahead went on this walk to breathe in the crisp air, but she is needed back at the house. She must make the scant breakfast, she must care for Woman-Who-Came-Before.

This is not a burden. Pine Mother cares for them. Corn

23

Mother cares for them. Earth Mother cares for them. Woman-Who-Came-Before cared for her. That is the nature of Mothers and their Mothers: a long line of ancestral tradition, stories told through whispers, ghost dances by the hidden bonfire, white garments on a black soundscape. For Woman-Walks-Ahead to care for Woman-Who-Came-Before, that is the wheel, that is good medicine.

Pushing her two braids over her shoulders, Woman-Walks-Ahead shifts the leash to her right hand. She dressed warm, a large plaid coat and a long-sleeved shirt; both have multiple pockets. She did not bring the bag for the medicine, but it's not the nature of the carrying, it's the intention behind it. Under her breath, she offers prayers to the Pine Mother. Glances up to the heart of the tree. Those silhouettes of the evergreens wave above her. The wind rushes through them, a palpable rush, a strong beat of a drum. During other walks, when she has taken the opposite direction, the wind has rushed through these weighted branches, these thickened trunks. As these weathered dresses jingled behind her, she thought to herself: *Is a car coming?*

No. Just music, healing music.

No car comes now either. She is alone with the Pine Mother. Bare hands gather up the needles from their mounds on the grey asphalt. She discards the brown ones. Her fingerprints shift to the texture of fresh molasses. Stickiness in strings attached from her nails to the needles themselves. The ends prick her. Little spots of blood appear on her palm, but she bundles them up. She removes a piece of twine from her jacket pocket and ties a handful into one bundle. She repeats this once more, two bundles. Brings the second one to her nose, inhales.

Medicine flows through them. This will help Woman-Who-Came-Before. It has to.

24

Woman-Walks-Ahead sighs and straightens up. Her calves cramp from the curl of her feet. She places one bundle in her jacket pocket, then steps off the roadside and onto the soil. The soil beneath the evergreens is laden with the dead needle-bodies taken by the storms, browned and loose. *Crunch. Crunch. Crunch.* She approaches Pine Mother holding her bleeding heart.

"Pine Mother," whispers Woman-Walks-Ahead. "Woman-Who-Came-Before is sick."

"Is that why she hasn't come to see me?" Pine Mother asks. Her voice, a quiet illusion, that tingle of numbing medication against the nape of your neck. "I miss her."

"That's why." Woman-Walks-Ahead holds the bundle of pine needles up within the line of Pine Mother's sight. The ancient countenance does not shift, but the boughs curve downward, in an attempt to embrace. "She's fallen sick. We don't know what it is, but it turns her lungs to glass, and her heart skips beats. This illness has locked down the world, and the Earth trembles with stamping feet."

"No." Pine Mother weeps. Great rivulets of sap seep across her breast. "It pains me to hear this news. If her lungs are glass, this means they crack."

"Yes. I ask to take your needles for a healing tea for the inside. I also ask to take your sap, for a healing poultice for the outside."

Pine Mother ponders. "I will do this. Woman-Who-Came-Before has taken care of me. She planted me and my sisters. She watered and tended to us. Five decades we have dwelled here, and four more shall we remain, despite the storm and the axe. That is the nature of the wheel that turns, all things connected to another. Asking and receiving. Receiving and asking." All of this, she speaks through her tears, in a clear, crisp voice, like winter.

25

The words sift through Woman-Walks-Ahead and her old blood. "It is so."

She cups the bundle of needles in both palms and bows as she extends her arms outward. She averts her gaze towards the muddied ground, the shifting roots. Pine Mother takes the needles and swipes them across her bleeding breast. Sap-blood stickiness, golden molasses, the winter's honey flowing from the comb. This golden ichor drenches Woman-Walks-Ahead's hands. She swallows against the tightness in her throat as she keeps her gaze to the ground. Some ceremonies are too intimate to witness, despite taking part.

"When Woman-Who-Came-Before is healed," says Pine Mother, "come and tell me. And come and tell me of this illness which locks down the world."

"I will."

Woman-Walks-Ahead takes her pine needles and Black-Wolf-Stalking, and turns back. The strong wind rushes through the pines behind her. *Is a car coming?* No car.

Blanched grasses line the front yard of the house with the chimney, which puffs smoke, indicating there is still life within. Two storey-house, tucked behind the guardian wall of evergreen trees. Evergreens are planted and tended, then grow to shield, to protect.

Some pine trees mimic. They pretend to be the Pine Mother, but are tricksters. Offering toxic needles, toxic tea. Woman-Walks-Ahead thinks about this in relation to the locked-down world. About how pine tar applied to the skin heals surface wounds, needles with boiled water provide relief for the glass of the innards. Decongestant and stimulant. Properties within, without. She considers this, and then puts it aside for later. Healing requires focus, a relinquishment of the self. Woman-Walks-

26

Ahead will relinquish herself for the sake of Woman-Who-Came-Before. For she would not be able to walk ahead, if there hadn't been a woman who came before.

Walking up the gravel drive, a gentle snake's spine of a curve. Entering through the garage door, scuffing boots and wiping paws off on the floor mat. Woman-Walks-Ahead does not pause to remove her outerwear, nor the leash from Black-Wolf-Stalking. Pine Mother's gift matters the most out of every task that awaits her.

Sock-clad feet shuffle through the mudroom. She manoeuvres down the small corridor, then finds the stairs leading to the lower floor. One flight of stairs, two landings. Walks on her tiptoes, holds her breath, cups her other hand beneath the dripping sap so that there is no spillage. Black-Wolf-Stalking pauses at the top of the stairs, sits upon his haunches, head cocked to one side. Humans are so fragile, despite their protests.

Downstairs, Woman-Who-Came-Before slumbers in the recliner. Brown-hair peppered with silver, pulled back in a low bun, loosened from her tossing. Dressed warm in layers, with a handwoven blanket from Woman-Elder over her lap. Feet extended and propped up, elevated to encourage blood-flow. Woman-Walks-Ahead remains quiet as she goes to the small kitchen. It has no stove, no dishwasher, but a kettle and a portable burner, which is good enough.

Earthen cup placed on the countertop. Electric kettle filled with well water. Press the button to boil. The kettle whistles. She takes out the first bundle of needles and sets them in the basin of the kettle. Young, fresh needles. No brown-stains. Make the black salve as the tea brews: black salve found in the cabinets of Woman-Elder. A container of tallow, scooped from the old remnants of last week's mutton stew. Black salve takes more time than tea. Herbs and oil in a tin, then melting the tallow, then stirring the tar into the tallow. She does all of this with the portable burner beneath the sink, and gives thanks.

The tea brews. The salve heats. She pours the salve into a metal tin to let it cool. The salve will be used later. Washes her hands of the pine-sap, the life-beating essence. Gives thanks as she gives it back to the water which nurtured the Pine Mother. The pine needles sink to the bottom of the kettle. She sets a metal strainer over the earthen cup, and pours the tea.

Woman-Who-Came-Before stirs.

Woman-Walks-Ahead takes the tea and brings it to Woman-Who-Came-Before. She holds it up to her mouth and lets her drink.

"This is a gift from the Pine Mother," she says.

"Hmm." A rattling cough. "Pine Mother remembers?"

"Pine Mother remembers. She remembers how you took care of her."

"And now, look at you. Taking care of me. I should be taking care of myself."

"You shouldn't," answers Woman-Walks-Ahead. "You cared for Pine Mother, so she cares for you. You cared for me, so I care for you. This is the wheel of things."

"It is so."

Another cough, another sip. Woman-Walks-Ahead adjusts the blanket over her lap as Black-Wolf-Stalking comes down the stairs. He lies down at Woman-Who-Came-Before's feet, provides heat and weight on top of the fur-lined moccasins. Sunlight pours through the window across from their figures. She will tend the fire, make the salve, cook the meals. Outside the house with the chimney and the snake-gravel-drive, the wind blows through the pines that guard the road, evergreen, ever-growing.

About the author

Enna Horn is a multiethnic author and poet who uses their writings as a method of exploring the complicated nature of mixed identities, inspired by the journeys of their friends, their family, and themself. They have fifteen publications in literary journals such as *Ayaskala, Emergent Literary Journal, BS/WS Zine, Yuzu Press Lit,* and more. A graduate from Indiana University Bloomington with a B.A. in English, specialising in Gothic literature, they currently reside on a hay farm in the midwestern tristate. They are the proud owner of several horses, dogs, and cats. Sometimes, they can be found lurking on Twitter @inkhallowed.

As She Lay in That Green Dress from M&S

Hannah Retallick

"You remember this one, though, don't you, my love? Barbara Streisand. You remember, don't you? Of course you do."

While Jacob remained kneeling beside the bed with his knees supported by a flat pillow, the carer had a hand on his hunched shoulder. In his left hand, he held the old MP3 player that one of his six grandchildren had passed down to him; it crooned painfully in the sanitised room of Trewartha Nursing Home. Jacob smoothed down the sheet that covered Barbara, who lay unconscious – his own Barbara – and then rested his hand on her warm stomach.

He turned to the young carer, who wore a black cotton face mask underneath a smudgy plastic visor, and muttered, "I'm sorry, sweetheart, I can't wear this anymore."

Leaning over, bringing herself closer to his hearing-aided ear, she said, "Of course, Mr Roberts. I understand. You do whatever you need to do right now."

"I really can't, I'm sorry." He popped off his disposable mask and let it drop to the floor; she picked it up, folded it, and put it in the pocket of her white protective suit.

"Barbara? You know this one, don't you?"

"She does, I'm sure?" The carer glanced towards the door, as though waiting for backup or fearing that someone might burst in at any moment. "I'm sure she does. Err, it's a lovely song."

"Barbara Streisand. *A Star is Born.* Do you know it?"

"Mr Roberts, you—"

"Our wedding song. She loves it, always dances, even tries to sing." A smile crept onto his tired mouth, his tone lightening. "Tries."

"Oh," said the carer, looking puzzled. "Not a good singer, then?"

"Sweetheart… I'm sorry, I don't know your name."

"Sophie."

"Sophie." He shook her hand, lingering for a moment to glance at her crinkled latex gloves and his own crinkled bare hands. "It is lovely to meet you, Sophie."

"You too."

"Well, I suppose we have already met. Anyway, Sophie, what was I saying?"

"Your wife wasn't a good singer?"

"Sweetheart." Jacob spoke with deliberation, as though trying to explain a complicated equation to a maths student of less-than-average intelligence, something he'd had to do many times over the years. "My lovely wife – still so lovely, is she not? – my lovely wife is the worst singer I have ever heard in my whole long life. Yes, a very long life. How old would you say? Guess, Sarah."

"Sophie."

"My apologies, Sophie. How old do I look?"

"Oh, um…" She frowned. "Um."

"Eighty-eight. Four score years and eight. Or five score years minus twelve. Yes, I prefer it that way, don't you? It sounds ancient, perhaps, but distinguished."

At that moment, another carer knocked gently and entered before either of them could respond. "You okay, Soph?" he whispered. He was a gangly young man who'd had to bend his head to get into the room.

Sophie nodded, silent, and readjusted her face mask.

"Can I have a word?"

She stood, slowly, her knees crackling, and left the room with him; Jacob barely seemed to notice.

"Yes, you enjoy singing, don't you, my love," he said, patting his wife's hand.

Barbara lay on her back with her eyes closed. Her arms were both straight, stretched out over the white sheets, pinning them like a paperclip. Jacob ran his hand up and down the arm on his side, squeezing gently every now and then. He studied her face. There was a map of wrinkles across her sunken cheeks and flakes of dead skin that had dropped from her brow onto her pale, almost translucent, eyelashes.

Sophie crept back in, this time remaining by the door, and Jacob grunted with the effort to turn and speak to her. "Sarah, would it be possible for you to make my wife a cup of tea? I am sorry to bother you, but she hasn't had anything to drink for quite a while and her lips look dry."

"Mr Roberts…"

"Coffee would suffice, if the tea here is… Well, I am afraid she is a little fussy when it comes to tea. I remember once when we were on a train from London to Glasgow to visit our eldest grandson at university – studying mathematics, I'm pleased to say, and he graduated with First-class honours… What was I saying?"

She didn't reply but returned to his side.

"Ah, yes, the train. My wife took a sip from the cardboard cup, nudged me, and said, 'Darling, is this tea or coffee? I really can't tell!' We laughed and laughed. I really can't tell, she said! She was always like that. We met when we were sixteen years old, in school. I'm afraid I tied her pigtails to the seat rail on the school bus, and yet, fool that I am, instantly regretted it and she caught me trying to untie them. I expected the verbal lashing I deserved and was shocked when she simply laughed and pushed my shoulder away, not roughly but playfully, and that was when I knew she had an excellent sense of humour as well as beautiful red hair – *Anne of Green Gables*-esque, one might say –

and I still see her like that even though all these years have..." His voice faded. "Barbara? I... Barbara."

"They're here," said Sophie, gently. "Mr Roberts. Jacob?"

She could have told him sooner; they had arrived a short while ago, but she stalled them. He needed more time, and needed Sophie too, needed her gloved hand on his shoulder as he looked down at his wife in her green dress. It was Emerald in the 90s when they picked it up in a Marks and Spencer January sale; faded to something like a mossy shade in the early noughties; and now, it was more like her eyes, the colour they would have been if they hadn't fallen shut.

He looked up at Sophie, confused; it was as though he'd never seen her before or couldn't remember how conversations were meant to work.

"Excuse me, sweetheart, what did you say?"

She looked down at the scuffed carpet.

Jacob suddenly grabbed his wife's hand again, gripped it hard; had he not noticed before? The skin whitening, her body growing cold, the devastating words spoken in his ear as Barbara's face had drained...

"I'm afraid she's gone," said Sophie. "I'm so sorry."

Jacob shook his head, frantically pressing the MP3 buttons, moving it from track to track and playing only a second of each, until he found the right song.

"You remember this one, though, don't you, my love? Barbara Streisand. You remember, don't you? Of course you do."

Dark suits entered, in solemn respect, accompanied by one of Jacob's daughters and the grandson who had graduated from Glasgow university with First-class honours. They began to well up as they saw Barbara – Mum, Grandma – lying there, so still.

"Oh," whispered Jacob. "Yes. Yes, I understand now."

33

Sophie reached underneath her visor and pinged the black mask off, revealing chapped lips, a worn expression, and the trails in her makeup from seeping eyes.

"I'm sorry for your loss, Jacob," said Sophie, placing her hand on his shoulder once more. "So sorry. Can I... make you a cup of tea?"

About the author
Hannah Retallick is from Anglesey, North Wales. She was home-educated and then studied with the Open University, graduating with a first-class BA (Honours) Arts and Humanities (Creative Writing and Music) degree, before passing her creative writing MA with distinction. Her work has been shortlisted/placed in several international competitions.

www.hannahretallick.co.uk/about

34

A Tear in the Cloud

Malina Douglas

Hugh leaned toward Laura, his face twisting into a scowl.

"We're in the House of Peace," he hissed. "You can't raise your voice like that."

"Oh stop it," said Laura. "You're always reprimanding me. We need to make the transfer before we sleep."

"Just leave it," snapped Hugh. "We can do it in the morning. It's fine." From their room of dark wood furnishings, he stepped into the bathroom and began to brush his teeth.

"It's not fine—" But Laura's words were drowned by the sound of the toothbrush.

Laura stood, mouth open, about to speak but was left in an empty room. She closed her mouth. The emotions churned on within her, unexpressed. It *was* a pressing matter. She wanted him to acknowledge that, to ease with his soft words the burden on her mind. But he would not. He was blindly convinced it was unimportant. He could not feel the urge that churned in her gut to resolve it.

The persistent unmet need burned on, even after they climbed into bed and pulled the wool blankets over them.

She wanted him to put his arm around her – it would not solve the matter, but at least it would be something, a little sign he cared. Instead, he turned his back to her. She lay awake for a long time, the wheels of her mind churning, spinning anxiety, doubt, confusion. Hugh's closed stiff form had already sunk into dreamland, worlds away.

They'd arrived at the monastery's blue and white arch the day before. The guard let them in, and they drove down a lane lined with slender trees and pots of red flowering cacti. The auto rickshaw stopped below a flight of stone steps. Peering through the rickshaw's tiny window, Laura looked up and saw a building with a pure white façade, its surface filled with windowpanes, the upper ones arrayed into fan shapes. Above the double doors was a miniature roof with red tiles.

"Come on, let's go," said Hugh's voice beside her. Over their seven hour bus ride he'd missed lunch, and his mood was foul. Laura was in no fine mood herself.

"Alright," she groaned, squeezing out of the rickshaw and pulling her suitcase after her. She had to crouch to ease it free.

Hugh pushed open the double doors and strode in. His loud boots echoed. They found themselves in a long foyer, facing a sofa and chairs with plush red cushions. On the small table lay a selection of newspapers. The walls were a yellowish off-white. Down the centre of the room were a series of columns painted peach and embellished with gold leaves.

Hugh strode through the cream double-paned doors calling out, answered only by silence.

Laura peeked into the foyer and let him go. She returned to the steps, where she sat with her suitcase. She rubbed her forehead. The ride up from Salem had been formidable. "A lovely place in the hills," she'd been told. She'd pictured the hills as the little English sort, not the huge stony heights the bus had ploughed up at full speed.

At each bend was placed a thoughtful sign. "Hairpin turn, 9/20" one said. *Twenty hairpin turns*, she'd thought with an inward groan. Just knowing made it worse. She'd craned her neck out the window, seen a high, verdant ridge, a few white buildings clustering atop it. *So we're going up* there. It made her feel weak just thinking about it. She turned to Hugh, but he was absorbed in his usual podcast. Environmental politics, a subject as worn out as an old pair of boots. She would have to put up with him talking about it for ages after. Why suffer to sit through it, too? She pulled out her book, a period romance about two sisters in India seeking husbands in the time of the British Raj. "Codswallop", Hugh had called it. Laura had defended it stoutly, then given up at Hugh's complete unwillingness to give merit to literature that was not bristling with facts.

She noticed Hugh's disapproving glance but read on anyway, a small act of defiance. *Is this what our marriage has come to, a series of small defiances?*

The bus stopped. Laura looked up, frowning. In front of them was the green nose of another bus but the road had narrowed. It didn't look big enough for both.

A man standing alongside the other bus waved. The bus backed up. They inched forward, the driver pressing as close as he could to the metal rail, lined with monkeys, a quite blasé audience. The other bus pressed close to the rock wall. They passed. If Laura stuck her hand out the window, she could scrape her fingernails on the other bus's pea green surface. But her hands were twisted in her lap, sweaty, shaking. She breathed relief.

The roadside had grown dense with vegetation, cream-coloured umbrella flowers hanging. From time to time they passed fruit stalls, women in saris presiding over piles of oranges. Chipping away at the time with talk, or staring into the distance.

The bus twisted sharply and Laura grabbed onto the bar of the window. "Hairpin turn 12/20" the sign read. Laura groaned and closed her eyes.

"You should do more joint activities," their counsellor had said. Laura had agreed readily. Hugh had protested.

37

"She's not interested in anything I am," he'd moaned. Laura had given him a withering look. She'd tried to join him in various activities – listening to podcasts, badminton, chess – but every time he'd come up with some kind of complaint. "You're not paying attention," or "you're not doing it right." She switched her thoughts to drown his whining voice out of her mind.

India had appealed to both of them, albeit for different reasons. Laura was more interested in the cultural side, Hugh in hiking. But whether he was ploughing up soggy hillsides or Himalayan slopes, he kept the same dogged pace, regardless whether Laura kept up.

She winced at the thought of their first hike, a predawn slog up the rocks of Arunachala.

"You're wearing *those* on a hike," Hugh had exclaimed, looking at Laura's loafers with derision.

"Yeah… so?"

"Where are your hiking boots?"

"They're too heavy. I left them at home." She was glad she'd left those heavy, clunky things. The loafers were lighter, and far more stylish. But Hugh was immune to considerations of style.

Hugh shook his head like a sailor giving up a lost ship. "Now you're really going to struggle to keep up."

And struggle she did.

Laura rubbed her eyes. They were pouchy from a patchwork sleep on a hard hotel bed, her nerves ragged. Her body felt jarred, almost nauseous.

A woman in a midnight blue habit strode up.

"Good, you've arrived," she said briskly. "Welcome to the House of Peace." Her brown cheeks grew round when she smiled.

"Thank you," said Laura in a voice like a fraying cardigan.

38

Hugh stomped out of the building. "There's no one—"
he began. "Oh, hi," he said sheepishly.

The nun turned her smile on him.

"You must me tired. Come, let me show you your room."

The nun led them through the cream double doors. *She must be profoundly peaceful, untethered to a complaining man.* For a moment Laura envied her peace. *What am I thinking!* She felt a pang of guilt. Thought of Hugh fluffing her pillows and spreading jam on her toast. Of Hugh deriding the sugar content of the jam she made. Stifled the thought.

Their room, at the end of a passageway, contained a double bed with wool blankets under a window that looked out to the adjacent building. *Woollen blankets – in India!* Laura had thought at first but the cold of the night later proved that they were needed. Wooden wardrobe and desk, marble floors, en suite bathroom. There was something old-fashioned and grand about it.

"It's lovely," said Laura.

"Will you help me with the bags or what," snarled Hugh as he left the room. Laura lingered as long as she dared to.

While Hugh tramped off to explore, Laura took the steps down to the garden, a swath of grass edged with yellow-green hedges and squat prickly palms. The moulded concrete fence-posts, some sections crooked, were trailing with a vine of orange flowers like little flared tubes. She sank down on a blue-green bench to read her book.

She'd barely read a few pages when Hugh's loud voice shattered her peace. "I've booked us a hike," he declared.

"I never said I wanted to hike," replied Laura, turning the page of her book. "I want to relax. *You* can go hiking."

Hugh clenched his fists. "But Janice said we need to do joint activities."

Laura gave him a determined look. "She also said we need to talk to each other more nicely. I don't like your tone. Why do you have to be so *forceful* all the time?"

Hugh frowned and gave her a dark look. "Fine," he said. "I'll be nicer. We leave in the morning, five thirty sharp."

Laura folded her arms across her chest. "I don't *want* to go that early."

Hugh let out a sigh of exasperation. It reminded Laura of steam rising up from a manhole cover in London.

"Why should I have to convince you all the time? Getting you to go anywhere is like pulling teeth!"

"If you weren't so bloody forceful about it, I might actually *want* to go."

Their stand-off lasted well past dinner, which they took in the empty dining hall, immersed in an icy silence. Laura felt disturbed by the clatter of forks on metal plates and the unbearable noise of the ticking clock.

In the hall on the way to their room, above an unlit fireplace, Laura spied a framed quote titled *Love*. "Love is patient, love is kind," it read. *Pffft*, thought Laura. But the bottom part made her think. "Love bears all things, believes all things, hopes all things, endures all things."

But can it really? Can ours? She frowned as she walked to their room.

At some ungodly hour, Hugh's alarm pierced Laura's sleep. He sprang out of bed like a goat and began to get dressed. Laura pulled the covers over her head.

"Rise and shine, porcupine," said Hugh in a sing-song voice.

Laura groaned and rolled over. She heard Hugh, already in his hiking boots, stomp into the bathroom. She lay in bed till the last possible moment before Hugh would be seriously irked. Then she sat up and rubbed her eyes.

Hugh was doing press-ups on the cold tile floor. Laura yawned. She pulled her suitcase towards her, pulled out beige cotton trousers and a lavender top, and slid them on under the covers. She tiptoed around High, wincing with each cold step, and splashed her face in the sink. Shuddered. The water was ice-cold. In the mirror her eyes looked pouchy, her long face haggard. She sighed and went over to ready her day pack. By this time Hugh was dancing with agitation and in a few harried minutes they were off.

Hugh pulled open the stained glass door. "Whoa, look," he said.

Laura paused in the doorway. Beyond two tiers of steps and the grassed, walled garden, and past a long blue-black slope lay the horizon, revealing the first streak of dawn. Hugh put his arm around Laura, and they stood in silence, absorbing the band of gold. She felt the familiar weight of his arm around her and sank into it. Then just as abruptly Hugh let go and sprang two at a time down the steps.

They walked down a lane with high walls to a place where five roads met. In the centre of the little concrete bus shelter, Laura saw the charred remains of a fire. A man in a blue plaid lungi and hooded jacket huddled in the corner. In front of her was a small flat-roofed hut with a hand painted sign that said "Chai Stall". Laura was intrigued by the mailbox, a rusted red cylindrical thing attached to the wall with a tiny metal door at the bottom.

The old man in the chai shop grinned, displaying white teeth. "Your guide is on the way," he said. "You want chai?"

There was only one plastic stool. Laura sat while Hugh stood, gazing out at the high-walled lanes. He was far away on the next horizon, somewhere she could not reach him. *How could I have nothing to say to him?* She felt emptiness,

41

and arising from that, despair, mingling with gratitude for the chai now warming her hands.

"Chai's good isn't it," she said to break the silence between them. Beneath those words, a small forlorn voice was saying, *I want to reach out to you, I want to connect with you.*

"Yeah," grunted Hugh, and in his short abrupt answer she heard him saying *you're not going to reach me and you're foolish to try.*

Before she could say more, their guide strolled up, enveloping their hands in strong handshakes and smiling.

Then the game was on, and they morphed into the agreeable British couple. Their guide Kumar, a sturdy strong man, led them past a colonial manor and began to explain its history. The House of Peace, he told them, was built by a British family. Laura imagined children running down the stairs to the lawn.

Hugh asked questions and soon launched into a discussion of history and politics. Their talk darted avidly from the ancient trade routes to sieges to failed expeditions. An irked Laura trailed after them.

They hiked down a hill and across a stream, lined with ferns, angel's trumpet with its deadly umbrella-shaped flowers, and cardamom plants.

"What does a cardamom plant look like?" asked Laura, scrunching up her face in puzzlement.

"That one, with the large leaves," pointed Kumar. "And these are silver oaks." He indicated a mass of tall straight trees with silvery foliage. "The pepper vine grows up the sides of it and the villagers harvest it from ladders."

They continued down the slope until the forest opened up to large slab of a rock sloping down to a village. A blue house, a pink house, banana trees, a stream.

42

"If we're lucky, we might catch sight of the wild gaur," said their guide.

"Wild *what?*" asked Laura, but their guide had already stridden up to a group of women. They wore long skirts in simple printed cotton and shawls. They were holding jugs, elegant the way the rims narrowed at the neck and flared, except that the jugs were of red and blue plastic. He spoke to them in Tamil, a series of quick sounds and a lot of "ah"s that Laura couldn't catch.

Kumar turned back to them, grinning. "One of the girls is going to the spring. She can lead us."

The girl turned to smile at them in a flash of white teeth.

Her slim frame was clad in a yellow collared school shirt and tan skirt with light print. Her black hair was looped in two braids.

She crossed the rock and slipped into an opening in the foliage, where there was a slim dirt track they would never have seen.

"These are coffee bushes," said their guide with a wave to the waist-high bushes. "See the berries?"

Laura brushed a red berry with her fingertips. *Amazing to think a coffee bean is in there.*

The girl strode ahead with sure bare feet, followed by Hugh and Kumar. Laura dashed forward to keep up.

All around them were silver oaks, some wrapped in pepper vines as if they wore shaggy cloaks.

Hugh, she noticed, was silent.

Morning sunlight slanted through the high oak leaves, dappling the path and the dark glossy leaves of the coffee bushes.

"It's beautiful, isn't it," said Hugh softly, and Laura saw the sunlight had affected him – it had shone through his crusty exterior to reach his heart.

She was transported to a moment, seven years ago,

when they'd strolled in the lake country, and he'd said those words. It was awe in the presence of nature that had brought them together, and she had forgotten that, amidst the flurry of stresses that were tearing them apart.

"Over here, look." Kumar had skipped off the path and was beckoning them in a stage whisper. He pointed to the ground. "Gaur spoor," he declared happily. He poked a stick in it. "Fresh, too!"

Laura squinted at the droppings on the ground. "What do they look like?"

"They're this big," said Kumar, spreading his arms wide. "With dark hides and huge curving horns. If spooked they can attack. This way!"

The slender girl was already ahead, hips swaying as she walked.

They followed along the side of a stone building with a sealed door, to a place where the ground sloped down to a stone-rimmed square pool. The girl knelt at the edge and filled her jug.

"The stream at the village is for washing only," explained Kumar. "So the villagers must come here for drinking water."

Laura nodded. She'd seen a woman knee deep in water, a red sweater over her sari with the sleeves rolled up, clothes trailing through the water as she washed.

Hugh paced the area, snapping photos with his phone.

Laura watched the girl filling up water. *How lovely*, she thought. *But if I had to do this every day, I think it'd be rather annoying.*

Kumar looked around. "Looks like no gaur today."

Laura was secretly glad.

Kumar led them back to the village and through it, down a narrow stone ledge over the stream. The woman in the stream was still washing, squatting as she beat laundry against the rocks. The surface of the water swirled with suds. Laura looked up concrete steps leading up to pale blue houses.

He lead them down a forested hillside, over large rocks. While Laura huffed and scrambled to keep up, their guide walked in sure easy steps, Hugh stomping placidly behind him. Laura felt each of the stones through the soles of her shoes.

They descended the rocks, covered with pale green lichen. She paused to touch it. It had a silvery glint to it, like frost. *We're on the rocks,* she thought, *literally.* She wanted to laugh out loud but knew Hugh would look at her strangely.

Laura turned; drew in breath. The hillside dropped away to a slope of boulders and golden grasses which descended to a tree-thick valley below.

They began to pick their way over rocks down the slope. Kumar marched ahead, resuming a lively dialogue with Hugh, while Laura trudged at the back. As she walked, she returned to a new and disturbing train of thought, in which she envisioned the various ways she would leave him.

Perhaps they would be in a chai stall, a roadside one, plenty of street noise. *I've had enough,* she'd say. *What?* Hugh would answer, leaning forward in that irritating way he did, because the horns would be blaring, and he wouldn't have heard her. And she would be forced to say it again, in clear forceful words, *it's over.* She'd expect Hugh to say something combative, like, *no, it's not,* more for his ingrained urge to take a differing view than anything else. This ending would likely be messy, drawn out. Laura would sip her chai too soon, scalding her mouth.

Or maybe they'd be in a hotel room somewhere. Laura

would be watching a film on her laptop and Hugh would be doing his own thing, likely tapping out something mysterious into his phone.

It's over, she would say out of nowhere. *The film?* he'd ask.

No, our relationship, you idiot. Except she wouldn't say the last part. It sounded far too harsh.

Oh but that's awful, she thought. *How could I be so horrible?* A bitter pang of regret welled up from inside her.

The golden grasses swished against her legs; stirred up memory. Santorini, cliffs, sunset. Hugh's hand brushing her bare shoulders, the surge of joy that rose within her. The thought that flared up as the sky ripened peach. *He is the man for me.*

Her mind teetered to a recent argument. Words flying like barbs. *You don't understand me, do you? Sometimes I wonder why I married you.* The sting of Hugh's words. Laura blinked back tears, forced herself to look at the landscape.

From dark rocks patchy with lichen she gazed out to a slope with tan and green bunches of lemongrass, to a slanting ridge clothed in slender silver oaks, their leaves grey green brushstrokes. Beyond stretched a low blue spread of mountains, wrinkled as a coverlet, with clouds in its folds. The city of Salem was a faint spread of white dots below.

The sky was covered with clouds, woollen and silver, impenetrable. *The sun will never break through,* she thought. Laura narrowed her eyes. There was one small place, far to the east, where the clouds were torn away like tissue paper, revealing a thin line of pastel yellow sky.

She drank in cool air; heard the white rush of water. She made no response when Hugh came to sit next to her.

It was like a blanket, their relationship. Thick and

woolly and comfortable. But sometimes the wool itched. She wanted to wrap herself up and snuggle into it, but she became so cocooned she failed to see the world around her. She sweated, she got restless, she pushed the covers away.

If he pulled away, she would shiver.

She cast a sidelong glance to Hugh. He was lost in his own contemplation.

Or it's like a cloud, she mused. *Thick, cottony and protective. But then the hard glinting sun comes out and burns it away, and the footless skies have nothing to grab onto.*

Across the plains, clouds drifted. They sat steeped in silence. There was Hugh, right beside her yet impassive as a mountain. She gazed out, alone with her thoughts. *I don't know if our marriage is going to survive, but I'm okay with not knowing for now.*

Hugh took her cold hand.

Note: The House of Peace is a real place in the hill station of Yercaud, Tamil Nadu, India, and the place where this story was written.

About the author
Malina Douglas is inspired by the encounters that shape us. She was awarded Editor's Choice in the Hammond House International Literary Prize and made the Official Selection for the London Independent Story Prize, Fourth Quarter 2020. She was longlisted for the Reflex Press Prize and the Bath Short Story Prize in 2022. As a finalist in the Blackwater Press Story Contest, she was published in their anthology in 2021. Publications include *Wyldblood, Opia, Typehouse, Back Story Journal, Ellipsis Zine, Teach Write, Consequence Magazine, Metamorphose V2* and *Because That's Where Your Heart Is* from Sans Press. She is an alumna of Smokelong Summer and can be found on twitter @iridescentwords or at iridescentwords.com.

Ava

Maxine Churchman

I caught the faint scent of a perfume that transported me to the other side of the world. I lifted my head and stared straight into the eyes of the most beautiful woman I had ever seen. Her face, so familiar to me, I would know it anywhere. Yet it couldn't be her. She strode past me with barely a glance.

I stopped abruptly causing a man behind me to stumble and swear. I apologised before gathering my wits and turning. Her tall frame was the same strong athletic build I remembered, with all the soft curves in just the right places. She was forging forward, the crowd parting like the waves of an ocean around a regal liner. I followed in her wake, squeezing less elegantly through the early evening London crush.

"Ava!" I called. She turned her head but didn't stop. How could she be here, now?

I first met Ava at the Rice University in Texas where I had a placement for a Masters in biochemistry, having attained a First at Cambridge and subsequently winning a scholarship to study abroad.

It was my first trip to America, in fact, it was my first time outside the UK, and it was both exciting and terrifying at the same time.

Ava was a goddess in a regulation white coat; a lab assistant with a magnetism that us mere mortals were unable to resist. It was difficult to gauge her age, a few years older than me perhaps, but she seemed so poised and grown up. I was twenty-two and still felt like a gauche schoolboy in her presence, too shy and in awe of her to strike up any conversation, but occasionally, she would

48

pass me in the lab more closely than I thought she needed to, and my heart would pound in expectation of her touch or voice.

She spent all her spare time, and I suspect a lot of her working time, performing her own research and experiments. No matter how early or late I used the lab, she was always there. I began to suspect she didn't sleep or eat at all.

Her constant presence in the lab was a huge distraction for me. I had never seen anyone more beautiful or alluring and her intoxicating perfume filled the room making my head spin. It would cling to my clothes, so later, with my t-shirt on my pillow, I could dream she was in the bed next to me, her long dark hair, loosened from its normal constraints, fanned out around her perfect oval face, a slight smile on her full cupid-bow lips and a twinkle in those exotic dark-green almond-shaped eyes.

One day during spring term, I came to the lab early to catch up on some work. Ava was there, she smiled at me, her teeth white and straight. It wasn't a friendly, I'm-so-glad-to-see-you sort of smile, more a cat-that-got-the-cream type.

"Hello Ben," she said her voice husky and full of promise.

I felt heat flooding up my neck and face, hot needles pricked my armpits and between my shoulder blades.

"Um. Hi," I mumbled as I dropped my bag on the bench.

"How would you like to help me with an experiment this evening? At my apartment."

She swung the leather strap of her bag over her shoulder and placed a piece of paper on the bench beside me as she swept past, tapping it with her elegantly manicured index finger.

"This is the address. 7.30pm."

She left without waiting for an answer, but who was I kidding? As if I would turn down such an invitation. I studied the address written in loopy handwriting. I had been in America since autumn and had still not ventured far from the campus. I would need to consult a map and work out how to get there. My whole body tingled with fear and excitement. I folded the piece of paper in half and put it in the inside pocket of my jacket so it would be near my heart, and more importantly, I wouldn't lose it.

Ava did not return to the lab again that morning, but I found her absence more distracting than her presence. I kept trying to imagine what her apartment would be like, if she would have soft music playing and offer me wine. What should I wear? Should I take flowers? My hands shook too much to set up equipment and perform experiments, and when other students came in wanting to discuss the baseball game last night, I found I wanted to be alone. I left mid-morning and nursed a cup of coffee in the cafeteria, staring out the window while my mind ran freely through possibilities for the evening. The sun dipped behind a tall tree and I realised I was forty minutes late for my afternoon lecture. I decided to miss it completely and headed back to my room to shower and get ready for the evening.

At 6.45pm, I locked my door and headed for Entrance 18 near the tennis courts from where I was sure I could hail a cab to take me across the river to the address Ava had given me. As I passed the sports field, hope buoying my steps, I heard an anguished shout from my left and just caught sight of the edge of a bright yellow Frisbee before it slammed into my left temple. Pain and light exploded in my head. The ground came up to meet me, scraping my knee and shoulder.

When I came to, the world was pulsing with blue light and I was surrounded by a sea of strangers, some showing concern, others merely interested. Two medics were strapping me to a gurney.

"Wait!" I urged, trying to sit up. "I'm fine, I have to be somewhere."

One of the medics pushed me back gently. "We have to take you to the hospital, sir. You had a nasty bump on your head, and we need to check you over."

I was about to protest further but everything started spinning and I clamped my mouth shut against the queasiness in my stomach.

In the ambulance, I thought of Ava. She hadn't given me a telephone number so I couldn't call her. She would think I had stood her up. I pictured her sad face, alone in the apartment wondering where I was. As soon as I was released, I would go straight to her apartment to explain. The thought made me feel less anxious. Little did I know at the time, I would never see her again.

Until now.

If it was indeed Ava striding purposefully ahead of me, but how could it be – she died? I slowed my pace, feeling ridiculous, but just at that moment she turned, perhaps to check the traffic or maybe she felt my gaze on her. Our eyes met and she hesitated. For an instant I saw a flash of startled recognition in her eyes before she turned again and ran across the road in front of a bus causing it to break and sound its horn.

I hurried to the kerb. "Come on, come on," I urged the bus as it lumbered past. I weaved through the traffic, ignoring the angry horn blasts, determined to keep her in sight. She took a side street, so I doubled my efforts to catch up with her before she could disappear. As I rounded the corner, she was waiting for me. Her hand snaked out and caught my wrist, twisting my arm painfully behind me.

"Why are you following me?" she demanded.

"I thought you were dead, Ava. We all did. What happened that night?"

"The night you stood me up you mean?" She gave my arm a final twist before letting it go.

I rubbed my shoulder. "So it is you?" I looked at her, not a grey hair in sight, no wrinkles, she looked exactly the same as she did the last time I saw her: eighteen years ago.

She closed her eyes and sighed, deflating slightly. When she opened them again they looked moist. "We should talk. You got time for a coffee?"

I would be late for a symposium, but she started walking with long confident strides down the road and I hurried to fall in beside her. The side street was less crowded than the main route, but I had to keep dropping behind as we passed knots of people coming the other way. It made conversation difficult, but Ava didn't seem interested in talking yet. She sailed on majestically, adjusting her pace for no-one. I felt like a small puppy yapping at her heels as I tried to explain about my trip to the emergency department. After all these years, the guilt was still there.

We passed a glass fronted gym before climbing the steps of what would once have been a swanky Georgian town house. Ava keyed in an entry code and I read the names next to the buttons on an intercom. Next to the number 10, was the name Ava Green. The reports after the tragedy named the dead owner of the apartment as Helga Stein. We, that is, me and my fellow students, assumed Ava and Helga were the same person since the incident was at her address and Ava was not seen again. If they were not the same person, it would explain why Ava was not dead. It didn't explain why she hadn't aged though.

I followed her up to the top floor. I had to take a breather after three flights and could hear the steady clicking of her heels as she continued on. I arrived sweaty and out of breath to find she had left the door open for me. I entered a hallway still gasping for breath. There were two open doors to the left, the two doors to the right were closed and at the end of the hallway I could see a dimly lit living room.

As I passed the first open door, I looked in to see a good sized bedroom and for a silly moment, I had the notion to stretch out on her bed.

Ava was in the kitchen, the other room to the left. I guessed the two doors on the right led to a second bedroom and a bathroom.

"Go through and make yourself comfortable," she said when I reached the kitchen. "I'll bring milk and sugar."

The living room was spacious with very few items of furniture. The curtains were closed and four wall lights cast a subtle warm glow over a rather sterile and unwelcoming interior. There was nothing personal to give away Ava's interests: no photos or magazines; no half read novels or partially completed crosswords; no sewing or knitting. The room felt empty and a little sad.

Ava came in and laid a tray on a small glass table.

"This is yours," she said placing a plain white mug on a plain white ceramic coaster. "Help yourself to biscuits." She sat in an armchair next to the table. I sat on the sofa near my mug.

"So, where are you working now, Ben?" she asked.

"Really?" I hadn't come here for small-talk. "What happened that night, Ava?"

She picked up her mug and blew across the surface before taking a sip. "I don't really know. I waited outside the apartment for you and was about to go back inside, when the fire alarm sounded in the block." She placed her mug on the table and picked up a biscuit, turning in round and round in her hand.

I felt the anger rising and spoke louder than intended. "Bullshit, Ava."

She looked up. Was that alarm or excitement that flashed

in her eyes? She shrugged a shoulder. "What would you know? You weren't there." She raised her eyebrows in challenge.

"Why would you wait outside if you'd invited me to help you in your apartment? Who was Helga? Why was Chrissy Dewer in your apartment? Why didn't they get out? Why did you just disappear?" And the question I had been dying to know the answer to. "And how come you haven't aged in eighteen years?" I sat back, waiting for more incredulous lies.

She tipped her head a little to one side and narrowed her eyes.

I felt like one of her lab specimens and the room suddenly seemed chilly. No-one knew I was here. I pulled my phone from my pocket. "I'm just gonna text my colleague before he sends out a search party," I said.

She leaned forward and put her hands on mine, the biscuit she had been holding fell to the floor between us, unheeded. Her hands were warm and firm.

"I always felt there was a connection between us, Ben. You were my favourite."

A favourite what though? I clenched my jaw to stop myself speaking.

"You must have felt it too?" she continued while squeezing my hands. "What do you know of my research?" She sat back, steepling her fingers, pressing the two index fingers against her plump lips.

"Nothing," I admitted, returning the phone to my pocket, text unsent.

"Longevity, holding back death," she said. "My mother spent a fortune on plastic surgery to keep looking young, and then died of a heart attack aged just forty-two."

"I'm sorry," I murmured.

"It's no good looking young on the outside if your organs are old and decaying. For proper longevity we need to be able to regenerate. Did you know there are numerous organisms that could in theory live forever?"

I was aware of a few. "And you discovered a way to make it work?" I asked.

"I am the living embodiment of my success." She spread her arms and sat up straight.

"Then why haven't you marketed it? You could make a fortune."

"Well, there is a problem with my methods that would make it…" she pressed her lips together, "…unacceptable." She studied her nails; artificial, polished talons that made her slender fingers appear unnaturally long. When she looked at me again, her eyes looked moist, beseeching.

Something stirred in the pit of my stomach. "Helga and Chrissy, they were part of your experiment. They were already dead before the fire started. Weren't they?"

She nodded, sniffing hard. "A terrible error of judgement on my behalf. I spent ages afterwards working out what went wrong."

"But you murdered two people and ran away."

She leaned forward, her eyebrows low. "Murder is intentional. It was an accident." She enunciated each syllable, I could feel the barely contained anger and it made me squirm. "Anyway." She sat back, and I relaxed a little. "The result on me was nearly as disastrous."

"Why? What happened to you?" Although an idea had occurred to me, it seemed impossibly ridiculous.

"I reverted, ten perhaps twelve years, so you see, I had to disappear. And let me tell you, it was hell having to live my teenage years all over again. I left for Paris as soon as I was able to."

That accounted for some of her youthfulness, but not all.

"You've run the experiment again. Haven't you?"

55

She smiled that cat-got-the-cream smile I remembered from years ago. "I did and it works like a dream now. I use the workout machines from the gym next door to harness life-forces from multiple people and I can use it to control my own ageing." She placed a hand on my knee. "You can't tell anyone. It's not exactly ethical since they don't know they are donors."

"Does it harm them?"

"I don't think so: each donates such a small amount each time. It's possible their life spans may be shortened slightly in the long run, but then again, the exercise and the extra calories they burn more than makes up for that."

"So how does it work?"

She broke into a smile that made my heart beat faster. "I'll show you. Wait here for just a moment." She rushed from the room, leaving me to my own thoughts. What exactly did she mean by life-force? It didn't sound very scientific. Would I be dead like Chrissy and Helga if I'd got to her apartment that evening? And, why did she trust me with all this?

She burst back into the room like an excited schoolgirl. I was about to rise when she grabbed both my hands and pulled me to my feet. Her mood was infectious and I found myself grinning.

She clasped my hands to her heart and the softness of her breasts against the back of my hands was incredibly erotic. "Ben!" Her tone was earnest as she looked into my eyes, and I fought the urge to press my lips against the furrowing in her brow. "I think us meeting today was fate. I have been worried for a while about the problems longevity brings. I can't get close to anyone and keep it a secret. I won't be able to stay in the same place for too long, or keep the same name. I'm so lonely."

She pouted, looking cute and vulnerable. It was my cue to kiss her, or tell her I wanted to be with her, but I hesitated.

56

"I always felt a connection between us, Ben. Tell me you feel it too," she urged.

"I do," I admitted.

"Then we'll do it together. Stay young together."

She led me along the hallway and opened the door opposite her now closed bedroom door.

The room was much smaller than I expected, lit by a single unshaded lightbulb hanging from the ceiling. The bold patterned wallpaper on all four walls made it seem even smaller. There were two high-backed armchairs either side of some kind of machine with a control panel covered in dials and switches. It looked like it had been knocked together from lots of odd bits and pieces.

"It doesn't look much I know," she said as if reading my thoughts. "Sit here and get comfortable." She gave me two metal rods to hold, one in each hand. A wire snaked from the rods to the machine.

"It's really important to hold onto these tightly. The first time you try this, you will feel a little odd. A bit light headed. You might even fall asleep so I'm going to wind this Velcro tape around your hands to make sure you don't drop them."

She efficiently secured my hands around the rods so I couldn't open them, then picked up another pair of rods, flicked a switch and sat in the other chair.

"Just a small dose to start with. OK?" she said.

I nodded and belatedly wondered who else had sat in this chair. The machine hummed and my palms tingled. I would have dropped the rods if they weren't taped to my hands. The tingling crept up my arms and I began to feel tired. Ava had her eyes closed and was smiling. I closed my eyes and concentrated on the sensations coursing through my body. It didn't feel right, surely I should feel stronger, but with every passing second I felt weaker.

"Ava!" I called in a panic. My voice sounded reedy and she didn't respond. My palms were starting to burn and I looked for the ends of the tapes, wondering how I could undo them. My heart raced and the blood pounded in my head.

Suddenly the lights went out and the machine stopped humming. The door crashed open. Someone entered the room and shone a torch in my eyes. I turned my head away. The beam moved on and I saw the stranger strike Ava with a lamp base as she tried to rise from the chair. There was a sickening crunch and Ava groaned, collapsing back in the chair with a trickle of blood on her forehead. I tried get up, but the intruder wasn't interested in me. They clicked a switch on the machine and hurried from the room. Seconds later the light blazed back into life and I flinched. The stranger, a middle-aged woman with thinning grey hair lunged towards me and I felt too weak to resist. She ripped the tapes from my hands and used them to secure Ava's hands to the rods that had fallen in her lap.

"Who are you?" I asked.

The woman looked at me. Her face was sallow and pinched with dark circles under her eyes.

"A victim. Like you," she said. "You should get out of here, while you can."

She helped me to stand and urged me in the direction of the door. My legs were shaky and it took all my concentration to move them.

Behind me, I could hear the woman turning dials and clicking switches, and then the machine started to hum again. When I got to the door, I held onto the frame and turned. She was sitting in my chair, holding the rods. As I watched, her hair grew darker, thicker.

Ava on the other hand was looking ill. Her skin had lost its colour and her once plump cheeks were hollow. She seemed to be shrivelling before my eyes. I still felt weak, but I was so incensed, I found the strength to lurch across the room. I picked up the metal lamp base the woman had dropped after hitting Ava and I held it above my head. The woman leaned forward but couldn't leave the chair without dropping the rods.

"No. Please." Her large brown eyes implored me, but I didn't know her. She was hurting Ava.

I brought the base down with as much force as I could muster onto the machine. It sparked and spluttered. I hit it again, before falling to the floor exhausted, but at least the hum had ceased.

The woman leaped from her chair screaming. She kicked and hit me and I was too weak to do anything but curl into a ball.

Eventually she left and I must have blacked out or fallen asleep. When I came to, I ached all over and could not see out of my left eye. I crawled slowly over to Ava and used her chair to pull myself to standing. My legs were wobbly but they held my weight. Ava's face was pale and lined but I detected a faint pulse in her neck. It was then I noticed there was a concealed door in the wall behind her chair. It had been expertly wallpapered so it blended in, but up close I could see its outline. I squeezed between the chair and the wall noticing how the wall flexed slightly: a lightweight partition perhaps. I pushed the door open and reeled in horror. In the dim light from the doorway I could make out a stained mattress lying in one corner with a metal manacle discarded on it. The manacle was fixed to the wall by a sturdy chain. Bile rose in my throat and my knees buckled. I clamped my teeth shut and backed out of the room.

Ava had lied to me and I'd believed her. The gym goers had nothing to do with her youthfulness. How many people had she imprisoned and used? She was a monster and she would have killed me too.

Bright flashes marred my vision and I dropped to my hands and knees to avoid fainting. I managed to pull out my phone and I remember dialling 999.

The next thing I knew, I was waking up in hospital attached to a drip and monitors. A pretty police woman was seated by the door. She smiled at me then left the room. I closed my eyes and willed myself to go back to sleep. The door opened and a nurse came in. She checked the monitors, stuck a thermometer under my tongue and wrote something on my chart. She told me I had been in hospital for three days after suffering a severe concussion, several broken ribs and a collapsed lung, and that I should make a full recovery. She wouldn't answer any of my questions regarding Ava and said I wasn't allowed any visitors until the police had spoken with me.

A little later, a couple of burly plain-clothes policemen came in to take my statement. They asked me lots of questions and made me go over my story several times before a nurse came and told them to let me get some rest.

I discovered that Ava had been brought to the hospital, but she had given her guard the slip and was now being hunted.

I had no doubt she would move to another country, reinvent herself and rebuild her machine. It made me feel incredibly sad and very thankful to be alive. Would I have wrecked the machine to save her if I'd known the terrible truth?

For Ava, yes, I think I would have.

About the author
Maxine lives in rural Essex and enjoys walking and yoga. She has been writing fiction for a couple of years and has had short stories published on CaféLit and in a number of anthologies. Now she is retired, she hopes to dedicate more time to writing longer pieces including a novel.

Evergreen

Anne Wilson

In the summer of 1992, I moved myself and my eleven-year-old son, Robin, from the north of England to live on the island of Mallorca.

Home became the second-floor of an old three-storey apartment block on a rocky promontory on the island's southern coastline. The entrance was overhung with vivid pink bougainvillea and the driveway was lined with huge agaves which grew towering, cream-coloured flower heads. Our windows and doors had green wooden shutters which opened on three sides onto a tiled terrace shaded by pine trees. Splinters of sea in the Bay of Palma sparkled between the branches.

On weekdays, Robin travelled over the Tramuntana mountain range to the county town of Calvia, to his new school, *Seis Quarterades*, Six Quarters, confusingly named after the land on which it stood. He was very popular as the only English-speaking pupil in his class and one of only three in his year and soon began to be fluent in Spanish.

All over the island, restaurants and nightclubs glittered and shone with showy outfits seven nights a week and warm Mediterranean air smelled of expensive cosmetics and perfumes.

In one of the island's predominantly English-speaking areas I saw a gap in the market for nearly-new or pre-loved designer wear and, after running the idea by a few friends, I rented a premises in which to open my shop, calling it EVERGREEN with reference to both its contents and also the customers I hoped to attract.

My stock was on sale or return and I bought shop fittings and clothes rails in Ikea. Ikea was new to the island.

I learned that their first store had been burnt down by rival Spanish traders but, undaunted, Ikea built a second.

On the day before I opened, Robin and I saw a skip at the roadside with a head and shoulders sticking out. We rescued a shop mannequin torso in perfect condition and took her home to feature in the shop window. EVERGREEN seemed to be the perfect location to give her a new lease of life.

The local population was multi-cultural and my customers soon proved to be quite an interesting lot.

I lost money when the elderly mother of a Spanish friend came to look around and, not understanding the concept of sale-or-return, (Spanish people associated second-hand with gypsies) believed the shop to be some sort of charity, and helped herself to an expensive beaded top. Not having the heart to attempt an explanation in Spanish, I paid the garments owner myself.

I also lost money when a middle-aged, professional-looking Spanish couple came in. The Señora ignored my greeting and wafted about haughtily before saying something to her husband then leaving the shop. The Señor indicated, in good English, that he wished to buy a beautiful, French, designer two-piece. I wrapped it carefully in tissue paper, after removing the price tag which I placed to one side on the counter. He then picked up the wrapped garments, threw a few loose coins on the counter and walked out, ignoring both the label and my protestations. I hurried after him to the door and saw him calmly re-join his wife, neither of them looking over their shoulders as they walked off down the road arm in arm.

Again, I had to pay for the garments in addition to feeling angry and humiliated. Both the "customers" and I knew that the local Spanish police would not have supported my case.

An Arab lady quickly became a good client, wanting to

sell, not buy. Her clothes were "designer label" and expensive which was very good for display purposes but she always pressured me to try and get more money for them than I was able to. I confess I sometimes credited her account with more than her agreed percentage of the sale.

However, I also had many lovely customers. One was a Swedish air hostess who popped in when she had time between flights. I especially liked her clothes and, unbeknown to her, bought some for myself; the only problem was, she was a size smaller than me.

One English client, Jill, who worked part-time in a nearby estate agents was what could fairly have been called "living the dream". She had left her husband and three children back home in England in order to live with a millionaire on his luxury yacht anchored in the nearby marina; a lifestyle which called for a constant supply of glamourous outfits.

Another customer who worked in a local tapas bar was happily married to the Spanish policeman who had arrested her when she and some friends were picked up for being drunk and disorderly on holiday in downtown Magaluf. She still embraced a holiday-party lifestyle.

I made friends with a good-looking local bar owner from London, who picked up occasional work as a model. We sometimes went for a drink together after his shift in the bar and one night he persuaded me to go out with us dressed in each other's clothes. A memorable evening ensued.

Meanwhile, Robin was loving his new school-life and his new friends although the curriculum was, of course, different to that back home in England, and I did think some of the lessons sounded a little suspect. He reported one "history lesson" which consisted of the class watching a long film "*with Sean Connery in it, and a lady who took all her clothes off*"! I eventually worked out it was *The Name of the Rose.*

Time passed quickly and we overcame lots of hurdles as we adjusted happily to the Spanish way of life. However, a few months later, my tolerance was taxed to the limit when I unlocked the shop one morning to discover a makeshift bed had materialised between racks of clothes in the already cramped stockroom at the back of the premises. In addition to this, an assortment of men's toiletries were neatly arranged on the shelf above the hand-basin in the little toilet. There was no-one about. I locked up again and went to call on the agent through whom I had leased the premises.

It transpired that the owner, a Spanish business woman named Puri, short for purification, had a cousin living on the mainland who came to the island each summer season to work as a waiter in a nearby hotel. To save him money she always gave him a key and allowed him to sleep at the back of the shop. No mention had been made of this extremely unconventional arrangement when I signed the lease, but this was Spain, and I knew that this was a slice of Spanish life. I returned to the shop and rearranged the clothes racks to hide the bed.

Surprisingly, disruption was minimal. During shop opening times my mysterious lodger was always working in the hotel. The bed was made each morning and all that remained of him between shifts were the mingled smells of toothpaste and strong aftershave. I confess to some curiosity about this man, living like a well-behaved squatter, but we never did meet and one morning in September I arrived to find all traces of him had disappeared overnight. (I thought to myself, *I'll write about this someday.*)

Robin was becoming ever-more fluent which came in useful as I was facing the fact, I had no flair for foreign

64

languages. He was eager to discuss his lessons with me but, again, history was confusing. One lesson I found particularly surprising concerned Guy Fawkes, who was of course Spanish. Apparently, Guido Fawkes and his conspirators successfully blew up the English Houses of Parliament by means of the Gunpowder Plot, thus bringing down the government and becoming heroes whose exploits are celebrated annually with fireworks and bonfires on the fifth of November. This was not the version I was familiar with.

Running EVERGREEN meant I was also able to pick up some pocket money on the side, doing ironing; much in demand in a hot climate.

I ironed in the apartment of a friend, Patricia an estate agent, who generously paid me time and a half.

I ironed in San Augustin, high up on a flat roof terrace which overlooked the Marrivent Palace where Princess Diana and her young sons stayed.

I ironed in Portals Nous in the penthouse apartment of an elderly couple from London; an island of Britishness with Astro grass on the roof terrace, fitted carpets inside, and soft furnishings labelled *"Harrods"*.

I also ironed high up a hillside in Paguera, in the house of a divorced Spanish businessman whose poolside overlooked his Danish neighbours who gardened daily in the nude.

I ironed in Torrenova for a business couple who socialised in some of the islands best known restaurants and nightspots. She had wardrobes bursting with designer clothes and a dressing table overflowing with beauty products and pampering paraphernalia. On my final visit, before they returned to the UK, I accidentally knocked her double-sided make-up mirror onto the tiled floor, where it smashed. Coincidentally, I had exactly the same mirror in my apartment so I swept up the glass and replaced the broken mirror with my own. Only later did I realise that the two mirrors weren't exactly the same; my mirror's magnification was much greater than that of the one it had replaced. I have always wondered at her expression the next time she looked in it.

There was no doubt that British customers always cheered me with their self-deprecating sense of humour and their eccentricity.

One middle-aged lady, bringing the entire contents of her wardrobe into the shop for me to sell, confided she was saving up to treat herself to breast enhancement surgery. Before I had time to really think, I heard myself say, "*Oh, what a good idea, tits for tat.*" I was immediately horrified by my own joke but thank goodness she was British and we both burst out laughing.

My time in EVERGREEN generated many happy memories and English shores felt very far away when Robin and I walked along the beach at midnight, barefoot on warm sand, the tide lapping around our toes and the air heavy with fragrance from hedges of *dama-del-noche*.

About the author
Anne Wilson's short fiction and autobiographical pieces have appeared in over twenty anthologies ranging from mild horror through the supernatural to the comedic. Her own collection of "dark" stories, recently published, is titled *What If...*

Anne grew up along the north west coast of England where many of her stories are set. She also lived for some time on the island of Mallorca which fans of the Balearic Island will recognise as the setting for *Evergreen* which is autobiographical. Her first novel, *Sleeping with the Dragon*, an unusual murder mystery with a fantastical element, is set in Mallorca and Denmark with hoped for publication in 2023.

Evergreen Protection

Sheelagh Mooney

What I recall most now was the absolute shock. And rising panic, I was utterly blindsided. I tried not to dwell on it because thinking about it can still set my skin crawling. Knowing I had been living next door to this creep for over ten years and had never suspected a thing was not good for my sense of safety. Realisation dawned that I had made the all too common but costly error of assuming that perverts are instantly recognisable and don't come in the guise of nice family men living next door. Long forgotten snippets of conversation start replaying in my head. On first moving into my home my next-door neighbour on the other side, the ever-cheerful Anna, had giggled while telling me to be careful what I hung on the clothes line as underwear often disappeared from her line. She had no idea where or who took them, she said.

"So, don't hang any of your little sexy stuff out there," she laughed.

She seemed so upbeat about it that I thought no more of it. I had unknowingly moved into a very close-knit working-class community where there were few secrets and where many of the occupants of the area were intermarried. A blind eye was often turned to unsavoury practices unless they infringed directly on each other's enjoyment of life. And when occasionally some invisible line was overstepped, justice was severe and swift. Few people ever considered calling the police around here. Occasionally I would notice a broken window or raised voices and if I ever bothered to ask nobody seemed inclined to provide any answers. It wasn't the way I grew up but to be quite frank, I could see some merit in it.

My real passion was my garden, a hobby that grew so to speak over the years as escapism from a boring accountancy job. My neighbours laughed good humouredly at my rambling cottage garden tastes, theirs ran more to low maintenance crazy paving, decking and built-in barbeques. I hadn't ever planned to stay in the neighbourhood long-term; it was meant to be a starter home but as the years passed and my garden developed, I found I had grown fond of it and of my mostly salt-of-the-earth neighbours. That is until one morning whilst getting ready for work, just out of the shower and still in a state of undress I was searching for clothes in the kitchen airing cupboard, when I had the unnerving sense of being observed. I grabbed the nearest towel and swung around in time to catch a glimpse of a familiar dark head ducking behind the wall of my neighbour Colm's garden. I was stunned, Colm a peeping Tom. I had been so sure that my house wasn't overlooked, that I had become careless, rarely bothering to even close the curtains. When I later checked along the boundary wall, I found damage to the plants where they had been broken off to provide numerous and now that I knew, fairly obvious peepholes. Feeling sick I erected some old trellis from the garden shed over the dividing wall to provide some instant screening but he was not to be deterred that easily. If anything, he seemed emboldened now that I knew. For a moment I considered contacting the police but what would I say and moreover how could I live on here afterwards. I had no physical proof and I knew he would deny everything, I mean I had never suspected anything myself so he was a polished actor. I thought about confiding in my neighbour Anna, I knew that she would at least believe me but was hesitant because of the rough justice that could be meted out in this neighbourhood. The thing is, I liked living here, I loved my garden and didn't want to be forced to move away. In the end, I did nothing more than get proper blinds on my bathroom window and make sure to leave my bedroom curtains permanently closed. My sense of security was rattled though.

Several months later one Sunday morning on a rare weekend away I received a frantic call from Anna saying that she had spotted a man staring into her bedroom window from my garden as she was dressing for work. She and her partner Billy had immediately searched the two gardens but the intruder was nowhere to be found. I knew it had to be Colm. Anna was so upset that I instantly realised that she had no idea whatsoever of his peeping penchant. I still didn't share what I knew and to make matters worse they suspected a poor man who had recently moved into a rented house opposite. To my eternal shame I said nothing and the unfortunate man disappeared from the estate as quickly as he had arrived. I tried not dwell on how his departure had come about and introduced a few more safety precautions, getting an alarm installed and locking the patio doors and the windows when I was alone in the house. His brazenness was the most frightening thing, I had always assumed that an outed voyeur would slink away abashed and suitably contrite, well not this one. Equally strange was the smooth alter ego he adopted when I met him on the street, all smiles, waves and not a whiff of embarrassment.

"Morning Jean, lovely weather, soon be time for grass cutting again" or "your garden is looking great, don't know how you do it" he would call out jauntily, especially if his wife was in the vicinity.

It was such a virtuoso performance that there were times when I began to seriously doubt my own sanity. I avoided him where I could but living right next door this wasn't always possible. I read up on voyeuristic behaviour and learned that it was not usually a precursor to other darker behaviour. This was something I clung onto until one dark wet night when I was away and my friend Kevin had come over in the small hours to feed my cat. He used the side gate to go around the rear of the house and was shocked to be jumped on by a man wearing a balaclava. He managed to pull the balaclava off in the ensuing struggle to find it was Colm who immediately became very meek and apologetic when stripped of his disguise. Had he first imagined it was me in the darkness? When confronted he claimed to have thought it was a prowler in my back garden, a plausible enough excuse I suppose if he hadn't previous form.

I finally concluded with a certain fear this was something I would have to figure out alone. I knew I should tackle him face to face but to say I wasn't good at confrontation was to put it mildly. I didn't know how to, my background and convent education had taught me many things – but definitely not that. Ideas like putting glass along the top of the party wall flitted through my mind before being rejected as being too risky. What if a child climbed over to fetch a stray ball? I also knew him to be a litigious kind of person, someone who while failing to maintain his own property was quick to sue the council or some other public body for compensation for all sorts of imagined trips and slips on paving or damaged manholes throughout town. He had quite the history there. I decided I would, as my long-deceased father used to advise, wait in the long grass and meanwhile trust to providence.

At least when I was working in my garden, I was able to forget about him for a while such was its calming effect. I took the opportunity to plant lots of carefully chosen dense thorny evergreens along our shared boundary wall including beautiful large specimen shrubs such as oleander, rosebay and Irish yew. They were costly but it was well worth it for the coverage and protection they gave me. Occasionally I would have to rearrange the plants over the little holes that kept reappearing as he broke off strands of shrubs to afford himself more viewing points. I pretended not to notice even when I'd actually witnessed him inflict damage on the plants with his bare hands. It was now an unspoken battle of wills. The boundary area on my side began to resemble a mini jungle. As he broke off plants, I added new ones. Then one day it dawned on me that I hadn't seen my foe for a while and there were no new gaps in the plants either. Perhaps he was away or just maybe nature had taken its course.

One evening not long after as I was busy pruning back the oleander shrubs along the wall Anna called over and we got chatting. I invited her in for a cuppa.

"Have you heard the news about our Colm?" she said once seated comfortably in the kitchen. I shook my head carefully peeling off my heavy-duty gardening gloves and leaving them outside the back door. Even the mention of his name could still send shivers down my spine.

"Haven't you heard he's in hospital? Quite sick I believe."

"No, I've haven't heard anything mind you I haven't seen him for ages." I didn't tell her that I'd barely spoken to him in the past two years and I didn't see him at all unless he spotted me first. I scrubbed my hands well with specialised germicidal garden soap before drying them carefully and then filled the kettle. "You can never be too meticulous after handling plants," I said as she watched me.

"Yeah really, I wouldn't know to be honest, I prefer mine on my plate, preferably the pre-prepared ones from Tesco," she cackled.

"Anyway, seems he has developed some strange illness, with vomiting and diarrhoea and blurred vision. It apparently improves whenever he is in hospital, but every time he returns home it flares up again. He can't even drive now."

71

"Oh dear, sounds bad, have they any idea what could be causing it?"

"Well, that's the strange thing, the doctors think it's some allergy or poison but they can't figure out to what. As you and I know he is not a man to bother himself much with the use of cleaning chemicals or weedkiller so it's a complete mystery really."

"You're right I've never seen him working with chemicals or actually working at all for that matter." We both chuckled.

"No indeed. Well, the fall-out is they are now considering moving to that new apartment block in the centre of town, *The Evergreens,* as he can no longer drive and it's difficult to live around here without a car and with no bus service. Maybe if he got outside more and took up a hobby like you with your gardening it might help him."

"Somehow, I don't think Colm is the gardening type, do you?" I laughed.

"Too right, anyway he won't even have grass to cut when he moves to his apartment which should suit him well."

"True, Anna. Somehow, I'm sure he will make a speedy recovery when he is living in *The Evergreens*." I took down the biscuit jar.

"Tunnocks tea cakes?"

"Ooh lovely, yes please."

Filling the mugs, I mused to myself how sometimes nature needs a little helpful nudge in the right direction and will then take its own course anyway. But moving to an apartment block called *The Evergreens*. I mean you couldn't make it up, the delicious karmic irony of it.

About the author
Sheelagh Mooney: Born in Skyrne, Co. Meath now lives in Ardagh, County Longford, Ireland where alongside her husband she enjoys creating and developing their Eco-Gardens.

Sheelagh is a keen environmentalist and gardener who holds a B.Sc. in Environmental Studies and an MA in Development Studies and when she is not working in those areas, she is busy honing her writing skills. She writes fiction, non-fiction, travel and gardening articles and her work has featured in many publications including *The Irish Times, Irish Independent, Ireland's Own, Leinster Leader, People's Friend, Woman's Way, Woman U.K, Woman's Own U.K, GreenPrints U.S* and has been published in numerous anthologies. She has also been broadcast on Sunday Miscellany on RTE radio 1.

Scheurer's Green

Jan Moran Neil

Green? Don't give me green. God's colour it's been called. And don't make me laugh. Green – that's brought more than tears to a girl's eyes, I can tell you. I'm going to tell you a story all about green that'll make your eyes pop, Miss Nicholson, mark my words.

My name is Charlotte Dukes. That's a grand name, ain't it? Makes people laugh. Me marrying into such a hoity-toity name but in name only and that's a fact. Before my husband died I lived down Shoreditch way with him and our Louisa and young Edwin. When my man died, it was St Leonard's workhouse for us and I started life that way too, God help me. But now the kids are grown I works as a cook, as you can see, in this here St Giles's Poor House for the poor babies. Fresh pastures for me, so to speak. But this story's not about me even though it's polite to introduce myself, Miss Nicholson. This story's about Tilly and how she made a mint one way or the other for Bergie.

I started out as a fancy box cutter, but it was when I started working for Bergie – that's what we called Mister Bergeron who owns the factory where I makes the fake flowers for the headdresses – that I met Tilly more than a year ago. Same age as my Louisa, Tilly was. Eighteen when I first knew her. So I'm getting on a bit now at forty nine. I was the head hat and headdresser and Tilly was the head flower fluffer. She would fluff the fake flowers which sits on the hats and headdresses I makes. I makes the fake flowers but I didn't fluff. I don't do that no more. And neither does Tilly. Bergie worked us all to the bone but my belief is, he worked on Tilly's bones more than any of the other factory workers. A picture she was, Tilly Scheurer.

But let's put it this way, Miss Nicholson, Tilly was a beauty but she was always a bit green around the edges, if you get my meaning.

The first time I noticed Tilly come over all funny was when we had our midday stop. Bergie leastwise would feed us some bread and dripping. Tilly was dipping her bread in the dripping when I sees her hand shake.

"You not so perky today, Tilly," I says to her.

"I'm feeling a touch sick," she says.

"Not got one on the way, have you, girl?" I mean Bergie hung around Tilly Scheurer like strung beads.

"I'm a good girl," she says. "I just been coming over funny two or three times this year."

"You work all hours God sends," I says.

"I needs the money, Lottie," she says. That's what she called me – "Lottie". "I'm not blessed like your Louisa," she says carrying on. "Marrying her cousin. Sun shines on your Louisa." And she scoured her crust into the dripping.

It was then I noticed it. Her hands. Green.

"I know you knows all about the workhouse and I'm not ending up there, Lottie," she says forking the bread into her mouth with her fingers. Fingers covered in sores.

Well, she had a mind of her own did Tilly Scheurer. But I could sees all that green being shovelled into her mouth along with the bread and dripping. She had her work cut out on her plate. Bergie never give us any soap but none of us thought anything of it until the factory children started to get real sick.

Tilly dyed those fake flowers in all shades of green – apple moss, olive, forest green, lime and Paris green. That Paris green should have stuck to killing the flies only. All the rage it was – it being a colour – green – which is hard to get your hands on and needs to be mixed with yellow and blue and all sorts, God help us.

Them ladies at their balls, they love anything emerald green. As a matter of fact, Miss Nicholson, they are ladies just like you. Anyways, that stands out that colour does – now that gas lighting's taken over from the candlelit. Shine out like diamonds those women do – yet just like the plague, men come over funny if they dance with what they call these girls – "femme fatales". Fatal those women are and not for nothing are they called "drop dead gorgeous". 'Cos, much as like, the geezers dancing with the emerald greens are dropping dead, given time. But they keep old Bergie in good business.

It's not just the dresses in all shades of green that the hoity-toity have a passion for. They have green walking up their walls and over their carpets and in their house paint. 'Course gloves is the worst. And sleeves. Greensleeves don't get a look in, I can tell you. But it was the headdresses which was my line. And Tilly as the flower fluffer. Her hands were doing a lot more with the green than just wearing a pair of gloves. Her hands were full with the overtime Bergie gave her.

Tilly got on with my Louisa like an house on fire. You never seen such a couple of dark beauties. Two peas in a pod they were. When Louisa came home in tears one winter's night and shrieked saying Tilly had come over sick and needed me in her room I swear I thought it was a botched up abortion. But my Louisa says, "No, Mummy. Tilly ain't been carrying on with no one. She's as green as God's grass all over. Please go round and I'll fetch the doctor."

I leapt round there, Miss Nicholson in spite all that November fog. When I sees Tilly, I swear no one on God's earth could have been dying of a more dreadful disease. When I sees the poor girl she was green from top to hip to little toe, Miss Nicholson. Fingernails and all. Even the whites of her eyes was green. She says to me, "Lottie. All I can see is green. You is green, the walls is green, Jesus (who was on the wall) is green."

God help the girl. Green foam came out of her ears and nose and when she took her last breath there comes out green water like you've never seen before. When they did the 'opsy, every organ the doctor says – her spleen, stomach lining, lungs and liver and the like was green.

Arsenic. I'm not at Bergie's factory no more but the green gossip reaches all parts. They put arsenic in the works to bring out the brilliance of God's colour. So you are from the Ladies' Sanitary Association, Miss Nicholson. Well, Miss Nicholson, I hope you tell Tilly Scheurer's story but I don't suppose anyone will take a blind bit of notice. They never do, see. Whatever the hoity-toity love they get. In green bundles. All for the sake of high fashion and vanity. Talk about making a killing. But somehow and someday, someone always has to pay for all that green. It's just not natural. The Lord's colour should not be fiddled with.

Now your papers talk about my headdresses being pretty poisoned wreaths. And ladies the likes of you are still buying them, while all the while Tilly lies under the green grass and Bergie is making a pretty penny to this day. But me and Louisa – we put a fresh evergreen wreath on that poor cow's grave whenever we are able. So you ask me about "Evergreen"? Dear Tilly Scheurer – killed at nineteen like a sewer rat. God rest that poor girl's soul. Yes, Miss Nicholson – she will remain young in my mind forever.

For Matilda Scheurer – 1842-1861

77

About the author

Training: Royal Central School of Speech and Drama.

Masters in Creative Writing from the University of Cambridge.

Publications include her performed plays by her company Creative Ink for Actors – on the London Fringe and in Cape Town, South Africa.

"Death by Pythagoras" short story won BBC Writers' comp/Radio 4 broadcast.

Red Lipstick & Revelations/Indigo Dreams includes her award-winning poetry published in the Royal Society of Literature's periodical.

When This Is All Over.../Creative Ink – a pandemic anthology for the Rennie Grove Hospice.

Shakespeare's Clock/Cranthorpe Millner. Jan is available for readings from her poetry anthologies and novels.

www.janmoranneil.co.uk/blog

Evergreens

Sally Angell

Here they come up the tangled path, heads down. Not speaking. To anyone else, just two women of a certain age with that samey Boomer look. But not to me.

See the thinner one, shoulders hunched up to her ears. That's my Ivy, never good at stress, always needing support. And today will be stressful.

"What a sodding mess!" That's Holly, in fashion boots, stomping over the cracked paving. "What do we pay that gardener for?"

Actually, Len wouldn't take much. And when his wife got the Alzheimer's sentence he said so sorry, he'd have to stop. Holly doesn't know that. She'd just replace him with a stranger from Bark, or one of those other places on the internet she's so keen on.

Oh, there's the house plaque! I can just see the top of it, lurching up through the weeds and the muck. So that's what happened to Arthur's handiwork. A bespoke sign, he called it. Ivy's seen it too. Her white bob of hair flops everywhere, as she tramples nettles down to get to it. Some letters are missing, but there's no mistaking what it says.

Evergreens.

Ivy runs a hand over the warped wood and stands up, her face tight with frustration. How could something crafted with such love and dedication be left to rot?

Holly looks over, but quickly away again. She's right though, about the garden being a jungle. The thing is, Len knew the flowers I liked; my preference for perennials. He looked after the wildlife carefully, and made the area by the hedge a sanctuary to sit in. So I didn't want someone else that I didn't know doing the grass all wrong.

79

The two women are ploughing through the wilderness, keeping distance between them.

Holly. Ivy.

Ivy. Holly.

"Do names make us who we are?" I'd queried, when my husband and I talked baby names. Like the lines etched into our palms, prescribing the future.

"Probably," he'd said. "I feel like an Arthur."

My girls' faces are tense, as they mentally take in the house ahead. Will it seem different to them? On the top step, Holly forces the key in the stuck lock. As the door gives, both of them back off as if not knowing what they're going to find. A glimpse into the interior makes me feel funny, let alone them. As they brave the hallway, I sense the tension between them, like a tight frayed string.

Snap!

"I wasn't coming today," Ivy shrills.

"Oh yes you were." Holly smirks. "You never could let things be."

A flinch. "Well, *you're* only here for the money."

My hopes for them to start to behave like adults are disappearing.

"Oh. That smell." Ivy leans on the radiator to her left. "It's just the same."

"Could do with a deep clean. The whole place needs a revamp." Holly's bright, sharp eyes glint as she pictures a makeover of her old home.

I want to hug them to me. I want to knock their bally heads together. As always.

Two children.

Ivy: "You're so prickly and sharp. And horrible."

Holly: "Better than being all clingy, creeping, creepy."

They were still like that at twelve and ten.

80

"Sis–ters, sisters!" It was the popular song of the time. But Arthur's toneless voice killed it. "Never seen such devoted SISTERS."

It was easy for Daddy to see the squabbling as hilarious. He wasn't with them as much as I was. Long relentless days. It was me who had to stop the pushing, the hair-wrenching, even bruising. Surely that wasn't normal.

"Sibling rivalry." Friends smiled knowingly. We were all bringing up children in the post-war years, young women wallowing at last in our fecundity after no proper sex for so long. "They'll grow out of it."

But they never did. It got worse. So you couldn't say, Oh just a phase. There was always arguing, fighting, hurting each other with words.

Arthur defended Ivy.

"Daddy's girl!" Holly would shout. And to Arthur, "You always take her side." He did. I put it down to Ivy being the needy one. He'd missed her birth, not been around. But I wondered.

I stuck up for the other one, out of fairness. Or that's what I told myself. But *did* I favour Holly? She was the firstborn. When my little girl burst into the world, there was a holly bush in our garden. Holly wasn't in the Name Your Baby books in the early forties. But Arthur's fingers were green. He studied nature, knew the history of plants. In the shadow of war, this new child brought the hope of survival. So Holly was new life, an evergreen, something lasting and enduring, like our marriage.

It isn't that I love Holly more, I would reassure myself. And it was true. Both girls had an equal place in my heart. Holly with her rosy complexion and robust nature. Ivy, slim and delicate. They were just different.

Parents fall over themselves to not admit favouritism. "We love you all the same," my own declared righteously.

But sometimes there's just an undeniable affinity with one, or a good feeling because of circumstances when they come into the world. I know that more than most.

When Ivy came home from school in her fourteenth year, looking like death, a cold hand squeezed my heart. True, you only had to look at her the wrong way, she'd be upset. People were talking about her. No one loved her enough. But this was the day I'd dreaded. All we could get out of her was that someone in her class had said something about our family. Ivy was quite young-minded for her age. Girls were not as knowing then. But at some level she must have understood.

Then Arthur was pulling his tie from his throat. I tore at his pockets to find the pills he needed. Everything else went out of my head.

In the emergency ward I sat by his NHS bed, blaming myself for what I'd done. When the doctors and manipulations had done their work, he opened his eyes, and tried to focus.

"It wasn't your fault, Misty."

That made me feel worse. "I wanted to tell you."

A nurse came to check his oxygen.

"I think I knew." His breath rattled, and I held mine. "But it doesn't matter."

He asked for a cutting from the plant in our apple tree. When I brought a sprig in, the orderly put it in a cup of water and it floated. One of the nurses asked what it was. She smiled when I told her, said she didn't think that grew in this country.

Arthur never came home from hospital, and things fell apart. Again. I'd got my life partner back once, only to lose him again. And it wasn't just me. There were so many stories of the continuing effects of war. We must have got so used to bracing ourselves for the worst, to not having people or things for long, that if something happened years later, we almost expected it.

The girls weren't the same after that. The sense of belonging and acceptance in families that's there underneath, no matter what, was gone. They never asked me about *Ivy's trouble,* though stories were whispered. It was too serious to speak about. People didn't blab about personal relationships in the fifties. Not like today, everyone sharing details and even photos of their goings on. And my secret created a rift.

We did have a coming together of sorts, at Arthur's send-off. The pain of his absence made us wobbly and adrift. But it wasn't like it is in films, us all crying over each other, just a sadness.

Everything happened quickly after that. They both fell for the same boy. All hell let loose, and that was it.

Holly ran away to London. Ivy stayed home for a while. It's her nature to pretend things haven't happened if she doesn't like them. She retreated into her own version of the past, an eternally Enid Blyton childhood.

Holly and Ivy have gone into the bedroom. Mummy and Daddy's room, an adult separate world. But they're going through everything now, opening the drawers of my life.

"Here it is."

I meant to sort my affairs, get a proper lock-tin, but it's all stuffed in an old Cadbury's Dairy Milk box. A few photos. Their school reports. An insurance policy. The Birth certificate. Holly unfolds the crinkled paper. They stare at the registrar's writing. Where I was born; the date. Who I was. My christened name.

"No!" Ivy splutters.

Holly frowns. "How could we not know *that* about our own mother?" Despite the surreal shock or perhaps because of it, they start to giggle. I join in and they look round vaguely, still reeling at the realization that I was a person before I became Mum.

A Basildon Bond envelope is tucked under the piece of card that told you which chocs were which, raspberry ripple etc. There's handwriting on the envelope flap. *For Holly and Ivy.* Holly gets out her glasses, and skim-reads.

"Are you sure you want to hear this?"

"Holls. I'm in my seventies, not seven."

It was a saga at first. Then a mini autobiography, but still too much information. So I'd cut it down. And down, until it was just what they needed to know:

Arthur died in the war. That's what I was told. I missed him very much, and later started seeing a friend; Ivy's Dad. He was a good man but we went our separate ways. In one of those awful twists that sometimes happened in those times (no global web then), I found out that Daddy had been in a foreign hospital, had no papers etc. He had been very ill, and when he came home to us was still in recovery. Hope you understand...

"Gosh, it's a bloody wartime Mills and Boon," Holly says, at last.

"And I'm in it." Ivy blinks.

"Don't you want to know your real dad?"

"Arthur was my real dad."

I thought he might have been, but the dates were too far out.

"He loved you more than me," Holly was saying.

"What? You know Daddy. If he found a plant or creature that needed help, he'd nurture and protect it. You were strong and confident, that's all."

"I wasn't. They just expected me to be."

Is it my imagination or are they actually being nice to each other?

"I still can't believe it," Ivy says. "About mum's name."

"It suits her." Holly grins. "She always was a bit of a flirt. Do you remember that butcher?"

"Oh. He gave us cheap meat, though rationing had stopped ages ago."

What are they talking about? These daughters of mine, raised in peacetime, have no idea of those hard years, when nothing was certain. People reached out in kindness to strangers, and helped those in need.

When Arthur had come home on leave that last time, the end was in sight, so we thought. Life would go back to how it had been, pre call-up, just lovely normality continuing on, day after day.

A couple of weeks after he'd gone back, friends dragged me out to the cinema. In the break between films a message flashed onscreen.

"Will Mrs Clark please go to the foyer."

I knew. They didn't need to tell me. So sorry. Arthur Clark's regiment was out on an operation. No survivors.

I wanted to die too.

The next day's a blur. I was out, there was non-stop traffic and it was like I was someone else stepping off the pavement. Someone pulled me back and I remember being annoyed.

But I had Holly. And somewhere inside I wanted to go on. I wanted life. I could never go into the Odeon after that though, without that blackness swallowing me up.

Wait. Holly and Ivy are actually *chatting*. Holly checks the other contents of the box, and stuffs them in her shoulder bag. She'll be doing the admin, all the procedures that reduce a life to statement facts.

They go round the room, touching the things known since their childhood. The utility wardrobe, the dressing table. We didn't throw things away, my generation. We looked after our possessions, kept them safe, made them last. We mended, we made do with what was. We endured.

They move into the lounge. "It's not the same without her." Ivy sighs.

"It's tidier."

"I saw Frank the other day. He still lives in the area. He always felt guilty that you moved away, after he dumped you."

"*I* dumped *him.*"

"No, Holly. He left you for me."

"Is that what he told you?"

"I didn't want your leftovers."

Here they go again. I knew it wouldn't last.

Evergreens are Poisonous. The warning was printed on a box in Arthur's shed. I remember it worried me, because of the children's safety. And because they had been named after evergreens.

Holly and Ivy are outside again as far away from each other as possible. The only blood relative they have now is each other. This feud has got to end.

I'm near the gate. I don't know what happens but it springs away from its hinges, smacks into our Holly's face.

Ivy: "Holly! Wake up."

Holly: "I've broken my boot heel."

Ivy: "I'll take you to the station."

Holly: "You drive—?!"

They're breaking up. I find it difficult to tune into what they're saying. In the hospice I had floated, between worlds. Holly's visits were short. She can't stand medical smells. She'd be standing in her city coat with a scarf over her nose, checking her phone every second. Ivy came when Holly wasn't there. She sat by the bed, read to me, rearranged my locker, tidied the bedclothes, held onto my dressing gown cord.

And I just drifted, remembered the softness and the happy times, Arthur working in the garden for his rehabilitation. The girls' voices as they played. Kodak holidays, birthdays. All the good.

I can see the holly bush bursting through the dead undergrowth, ivy flowing over the ground. And up in the tree somewhere, there is still mistletoe.

About the author
Sally Angell's short stories and flash fiction have been published in magazines and anthologies. She has won competitions, including the H.E. Bates national short story competition. In her work she wrote drama scripts that were used for local performances. And her stories have been broadcast on radio. She has been involved with writing events for many years. Now retired, Sally enjoys exploring and writing for current markets.

Flower Girls

Tony Oswick

"Smile please."

As the photographer motions with his hand, Wendy and I edge closer together on the stage. I'm under no allusions. I've only been asked to be in the picture because I'm President of the Village Gardening Society.

The camera flashes.

"That's fine, ladies. We'll have that on the front page next week." I can see the photographer chuckling. "Well, perhaps not the front page but it's always helpful to get a pic to go with the Gardening Show report." He gathers up his camera and other items of expensive-looking equipment, and hurries out of the Village Hall.

"I'm glad that's all over," I say to Wendy, her hand still gripping the trophy. "I hate having my picture taken. So will you when you get to my age." Everyone can see I'm old but I never let on I'll be ninety-four next birthday.

She shrugs. "Actually, I've never minded people taking photographs. I've had so many taken over the years, I've got used to it."

Wendy Malone has won "The Best Newcomer Trophy" for 2012. Six exhibition roses. Apricot Silk. She's younger than me, much younger, but then everyone is these days. The photographer wanted a picture of someone attractive for the newspaper. Wendy, with her long brown hair and lack of wrinkles, looks forty-something but is probably much older.

"I've always loved flowers, Mrs Pearce." Wendy wants to talk. "Even as a child my mother said I had green fingers. Said I'd be a success whatever I did. When I was at school, my headmistress told me I was capable of anything. 'Never

88

cloud your horizons, Wendy,' she'd say. 'Go for it'. I've always lived my life like that. *Carpe diem.* That's Latin, you know. 'Seize the day'."

Wendy moved into Honeypot Cottage less than a year ago. I've said "hello" on a few occasions but never had a proper conversation with her.

"You've done very well, dear. They were beautiful roses. It took me twenty years of trying before I won something and then it was only a Highly Commended Certificate. Still, it's not the winning but the taking part that counts."

"I'm not sure about that." Wendy's voice is firm. "There's no point entering competitions if you don't want to win. I don't mean win at all costs. But you have to be competitive. Don't you agree?"

I grunt. People think it's something to do with my age but grunting saves me having to agree or disagree. Saves arguments, too.

Wendy assumes I agree with her.

"I've been so lucky in my life, Mrs Pearce. I've been all over the world, seen lots of places, done lots of things." She leans closer and touches my arm. "When I was a teenager, I promised myself I'd visit a different country for every year of my adult life. So far I've done forty-eight countries – forty-eight! And I'm not yet sixty-two." She steps back to await my approval.

I produce a smile. "That's very good, dear."

"Mind you, it helped because I was in the music business. I don't suppose you've ever heard of The Tangerine Girls? We were famous in the Sixties and Seventies. A backing group, you know. Never had any hits ourselves but we sang with all the big names. Cliff, Tom, Englebert – the real stars."

I wonder why she moved here? Will she find our village boring? "Sounds great fun."

"It was. There are a few stories I could tell. My second husband said I should write a book and call it 'More Sex, More Drugs and More Rock 'n Roll'. But if I did, they'd censor most of it." She laughs out loud. "I suppose you don't remember flower power and the Summer of Love? All those Rock Festivals? People said we were hedonistic. But if you can't enjoy yourselves when you're young, when can you?"

When indeed, I think.

"Are you ready?" A voice is calling from the Hall doorway. It's Cyril Margerum. All the other members of the Gardening Society have finished clearing the stalls away and Cyril's offered to give me a lift home. I wave to him from the stage.

"Just coming, Cyril." I turn to Wendy. "It's been lovely talking to you, dear." She kisses me on the cheek. "And well done again for winning the trophy."

Cyril helps me down from the stage and we walk to his car, parked in front of the Village Hall.

"The show went very well today," he says, opening the door for me. "Such a lot of beautiful flowers. Always cheer you up, don't they."

I nod.

"That's what flowers are meant to do, Cyril. But I'm starting to feel quite weary now. All this excitement has tired me out."

When I get home, I'll make myself a nice cup of tea – but I must try not to nod off.

I wake with a start and peer through the gloom at the clock. It's twenty past eight and the sky outside is greying. I must've been asleep almost three hours.

I turn on the table lamp which sits next to my chair. The light shines on the photograph of Stanley. My darling

90

Stanley. What a handsome young man he is. Even more so in his uniform. I keep a single red rose in a vase by the side of his photograph. Always.

"It's been a good day today, Stanley," I say picking up the photograph. "I'm not sure you would've liked it. Too many talkative women. But there were some lovely flowers. You would've enjoyed those."

I brush my lips against the photograph. It was taken seventy-two years ago. In 1940. That was the year I drove ambulances through London's streets. Streets of air-raid sirens and burning, bombed-out buildings. I remember feeling so helpless. All that devastation and waste. And suffering. It was also the year of Dunkirk. The year I got the telegram. I was only twenty-one.

I recall Wendy's words.

"But if you can't enjoy yourselves when you're young, when can you?"

I replace the photograph on the table and take a sip of cold tea.

About the author

Born and brought up in East London, Tony has lived in Clacton-on-Sea for over 50 years. After a life-time of work in the Civil Service and funeral service, he took up writing fourteen years ago. He professes to "write for pleasure" but admits enjoying the kudos of an occasional publication or competition success. He's a founder-member of The Seaview Scribblers, Frinton Write Types and Wivenhoe Shed Writers.

Forever Green

Jenny Palmer

"Blue and green should never be seen" was a favourite rhyme that people used to say, when we were growing up and were talking about what to wear. Or sometimes you'd hear the other version: "Green and blue make donkeys spew." It didn't make any sense to me. Blue and green were my favourite colours. They were the colours I saw every day. Green was the colour of the grass in the meadows where I played all day long with my sister. Blue was the colour of the sky when the sun was shining, and we lay in the grass watching the clouds drift across the sky. If they went together in nature, why couldn't they go together in clothing?

I often wore green, especially after Auntie Don bought her state-of-the-art knitting machine and churned out Christmas sweaters for us. I loved the chunky, olive-green cardigan she gave me and was sad when I grew out of it. It was one of my all-time favourites, along with the red sweater with the buttons across the shoulder that she had salvaged from one of her upmarket cleaning jobs. Or the second-hand, purple, winter coat with the fake fur collar that I wore when I went out sledging in winter. We never bought clothes then. They just appeared.

In my teens, I had more choice in the matter. I adopted the ubiquitous blue jeans as my go-to option and wore whatever sweater my auntie turned out that year. One year I pulled back an orange twinset that I had grown out of and re-knit it as a Sloppy Joe sweater. I thought it the height of fashion. My mother couldn't understand it.

I was still wearing blue when I lived in the squat in London. I was challenged on it by one of my housemates.

"You always wear blue," she came out with one day, a propos of nothing. "With your eye colour, you should be wearing autumnal colours like brown or auburn."

"But I like blue," I said. "It's my favourite colour."

I had never considered matching clothes with my eye colour. My eyes were hazel. At least that was what I had put on my passport. I was surprised that she'd even noticed. We were both living in the squat for financial reasons, but we were poles apart. She was a committed socialist feminist who was bent on changing the world. She and her like-minded friends often met around our kitchen table, where they spent hours thrashing out their stance on the latest political developments. I wasn't into politics in those days. I had just come back from a year abroad teaching English and was homeless. I was trying to get myself back on the career ladder and was only too glad to be living rent free in this semi-derelict house. After doing a professional development course, I had found a full-time teaching job in a private language school in Oxford Street.

My squat mate had seen fit to offer me the benefit of her advice and for some reason I decided she must be right. It was time to branch out. I soon found myself bowing to her superior knowledge and scouring the second-hand markets of Portobella and Petticoat Lane. It was at a time when vintage dresses with small grannie print were in. I found one in lilac and another in yellow. They reminded me of the dress my mother wore on her wedding day in the early forties when she was slim and pretty. The dresses didn't do much for my pasty complexion and I only wore them a couple of times.

Years later in the eighties, I went on an extended trip to South America. I was enthralled by the exuberance of the colours. Women wore multi-coloured full skirts and carried bundles on their backs in awayos of striped woven cloth.

Their clothes were in all the colours of the rainbow, and yet nothing seemed to clash. You saw orange with red and shocking pink, and green with blue and yellow, all in the same garment. This symbolised for me a different way of looking at the world. It was one I hadn't encountered before. I bought a small handloom and came back with my bags stuffed with multi-coloured, knitted, woollen sweaters. Punk was over in London, and everyone looked sad and dreary. It was as if they had gone into mourning. On the Tube black was the predominant colour.

On my return I took up weaving and adopted a South American colour palette. I wore my chunky, multi-coloured sweaters, warm and scratchy as they were and suffered in many a centrally heated London venue because of this. There were a couple of very hot summers in the late eighties. People said it was due to climate change. I had no further need for my sweaters. I left them hanging in the wardrobe where they were attacked by an infestation of moths and literally fell to pieces.

These days I live in the countryside again. It's not a conscious thing but I've noticed that I'm wearing blue or green most of the time and often the two together. I must have imbibed them from the environment. I don't play out in the fields like I used to, but I do go for long walks and sometimes I'll lie down in the grass and look at the sky. It's a habit I started during Covid. It makes me feel close to the earth and helps to keep me sane. I expect I'll be doing a lot more of it in future, what with the rising fuel bills, the threat of power cuts, the risk of floods and the ongoing war in the Ukraine.

You don't need a reason to like something, I've discovered. And you don't need other people's permission either. I like nature. I feel comfortable when I'm out in the countryside. That's it. And I'd like this planet to carry on for generations to come.

About the author

Jenny Palmer writes poetry, short stories and local history, inspired by the Pendle area where she lives. She contributes regularly to *CaféLit*. Her stories appeared in the *Best of CaféLit* anthologies 3,5, and 7, in *Citizens of Nowhere* and in her own collection *Keepsake and other stories*, published by Bridge House. She has published two memoirs *Nowhere better than home* and *Pastures New*, a book of poems called *Pendle poems* and two family histories, the latest of which *Witches, Quakers and Nonconformists*, 2022, is available at the Pendle Heritage Centre, Barrowford.

Green Spaces

Jane Spirit

Adrian adjusted his digital wall to view the photograph he
had selected from its nostalgia bank. He felt relieved that he
could manipulate his rather old-fashioned technology well
enough to have a reasonable stab at this assignment. There
had been several reasons to select this image of his great-
grandmother for it. For one thing, he liked the neatness of
her birth year, 1972, so exactly one hundred and fifty years
ago. Also, thinking about her had triggered a half-framed but
intense memory of his grandmother, her daughter, holding
him up high in her arms to point out something outside the
window of her flat. He hoped that this visceral connection to
his long dead family might make completing the assignment
easier for him.

As he understood it, he was required simply to study a
historic human image and write about his reaction to the
past it represented. He assumed that the exercise was
designed to encourage students to think about the changes
in their personal lives and circumstances as well as
historical change. In his case this meant adjusting to the
slow loss of his motor functions now that the "lifeboat" cell
re-genesis treatment hadn't worked. Fortunately, he could
still manage his day-to-day life and was eligible to have an
automatic activator implanted when he felt he needed it. It
was good too that he had been allocated a placement on his
employer's personal enhancement study scheme. Still, he
couldn't help feeling slightly resentful about some of these
early assignments. He had, after all, adapted quickly to his
physical deterioration and he was grateful to have been
born in the 2070s. If he thought about himself at all it was
as the flotsam and jetsam of the turbulent previous century,

bobbing in the calmer waters of the twenty-second. He assumed that this was the actual if unstated outcome intended by the tutor who had set this latest task.

Adrian had his misgivings, but he also had his schedule for the day. This assignment had to be completed before others could be begun. He would not prevaricate any further. He would look and reflect as asked. Initiating some quiet music to aid his focus Adrian forced himself to gaze at the picture of his great-grandmother Sharon, taken in 2022 when she, like him, was just into her fifties. Sharon was standing in what he assumed was her own garden, wearing rather too tight-fitting trousers and a baggy shirt in various shades of green and cream. Although some grey still showed through, her hair had apparently been dyed a light brown to match her hazel eyes. The brightest things in the image were her blue and white swirly patterned boots, presumably made of plastic. Adrian had seen some like them last year in his local Past Life Museum and been interested by the origins of their name: Wellingtons. He considered how there seemed to be nothing exceptional or objectionable about Sharon; perhaps it was the apparently comfortable normality of her world that made the image so poignant. He stared at her and at the ground patterned with almost garish green and brown leaves, like a worn exotic rug laid at her feet.

He was fortunate of course to have a green room in his flat with its own internal self-adjusting glass dome and temperature control. The variegated colours of its stems and shoots gave him pleasure as did the foods he grew there and shared meticulously with his neighbours. He wondered though about how it might feel to wander across an area of natural grass on which you could simply stand or sit or even lie down in the fresh air. He noticed that his great-grandmother was smiling in the image. Presumably a

97

garden with its own trees and plants and grass was a place associated with happiness.

He started to make a careful note of his feelings; an echo of what he presumed was some genetically encoded yearning for an outdoor world, but also pride that he could still experience some of its pleasures indoors within a modern Safe Space. He stared intently again at the image of Sharon, this time noticing the way in which her gaze was directed slightly off to one side, towards some darker green foliage on the edge of the picture frame. The nostalgia bank told Adrian that this was almost certainly part of a rhododendron bush and one that would in due course produce a foaming mass of showy pink flowers against its glossy leaves, green all the year round. It wasn't a native species, but grown, transported, tended, and admired simply for its sumptuous quality, its beauty. He reminded himself that a hundred years ago owning such ornamentation and having it all to yourself to enjoy was an everyday thing. He noted down his own excitement in seeing it, but also his feelings of faint disapproval; how could Sharon not have thought of using such precious outside space to grow food, even in those days?

As Adrian looked in detail at the lower part of the picture, he changed his music to replicate an appropriate soundscape. It was one that he would never be able to hear in real life. Even if he were able to walk unaided, no strolling was permitted amongst the few trees within the Past Life Museum woodland dome. He notched up the volume to hear the rhythmic rustling of the wind in the trees and then the scrunching sounds of trodden leaves. In his mind's eye he watched momentary flashes of clashing lime and pumpkin colours mellowed by the low-lying sun as the leaves were kicked up and floated back down. The replayed sounds and imagined colours evoked for him that long-gone time when the different seasons could be experienced in an outdoor place.

Adrian became aware of his own heightened emotion and controlled any imminent tears by regulating his breathing for a few moments. Then he calmly noted his final reactions, his feelings of envy and of longing, but also of anger and frustration. After that he re-banked the image, satisfied now that he had completed the required assignment and could move on. Sharon's world, fascinating as it was, would remain always unreachable to him. He was only a voyeur who could never recapture the essence of that long-ago life. More tellingly, he did not want to. Knowing what the future would hold for Sharon's world, he wanted no part of it. The tears he had restrained were not nostalgic ones. They had welled up out of an overwhelming sorrow for what had been still to come when the picture was taken, as well as an overwhelming relief that those events were now safely consigned to the past.

About the author
Jane Spirit lives in Suffolk UK. She has written academic articles and books from time to time and is now enjoying writing fiction.

Never Old – Ever Green and Good To Go

Allison Symes

They tell me I'm too old, I've had my day, and I should simply hang up my wand and have a comfortable retirement. They tell me I've earned it and it is time to take life easy.

Ha! You're as young as you feel is a motto I've always lived by and I still think my long years of experience as a fairy godmother still count for something. I also know I haven't given all I know I could give to the service of magic and the fairy world I live in especially.

It's just that the powers that be have decided otherwise. Since when has ageism been an official policy? I must have missed the memo on that one. Mind you, had I seen it I would have told them where to shove said memo!

Apparently the new boss, our young, glamorous and oh so shiny Fairy Queen has decided there should be a new approach to everything. Harrumph! Don't get me wrong. I'm all for technological change where that is clearly useful.

The recent automatic wand upgrade was a great idea. It's too easy to forget to take these things in for servicing and a flat wand is useless in a magical crisis I can tell you. Nobody likes their equipment failing the Wand Operating Totally Okay Test (WOTO). I think you have something along similar lines called the MOT but I digress.

Anyway I'm called in, told the above rubbish about hanging up my wand, and sent home. Yes, sent home just like a naughty kid (and boy can my colleague, the Tooth Fairy, share horror stories about *those*).

Goodness knows how many dragons and foul fiends I've taken care of for my people. I've thwarted a few evil wizards in my time too though there was one I do wonder about.

Looking back, I do think his dodgy intent was towards me personally, I did cut quite the figure back in the day, and I may have been a bit hasty in sending him packing. Oh well. It is true you don't miss what you've never had. And in fairness, I was preoccupied with my career then.

I have no idea what I will do now. Oh I'll get my garden sorted out. I've got books to organise, you know the kind of task you've been meaning to do if only you had the time, but after all that... then what?

And to just feel unwanted and unneeded is horrible. I know none of us go on for ever but I did feel I still had at least a good decade of useful service in me.

It doesn't help I've seen rumours on the news of another foul fiend lingering on the borders of our realm. The Queen says the magic spells she's put on the borders are preventing it from coming through.

I have my doubts. I think it is biding its time. I suppose it didn't help my cause I told Her Nibs that. Oh well. I can only hope she's right.

That bloody foul fiend has broken through Her Nibs' spells and is running amok in the villages around Claresbury. Over fifty dead so far and that's an estimate. They're going by body parts found left lying about.

I'm itching to get my wands out and send that beast back to whatever circle of hell it originated from but I'm retired now.

And the Queen has urged us all to remember as this is an endangered species, we are not to be too hasty, and the answer is to give it alternative sources of meat.

That would be fine if I hadn't watched it on the news deliberately taking people and buildings out for the sake of it. No calorific value in buildings as far as I know so why go for those?

I wonder how many have got to die before Her Nibs realises it is time to go back to old school magical policing and send these monsters packing. There is a time and a place for a kindly word but not when dealing with foul beasts.

Mind you, I can think of a fair few not so kindly words to use but then I've been around long enough to remember when these things were new.

I did tell the Queen you can't negotiate with a foul fiend. Evil flourishes like the green bay tree, I told her. I know it's one of your sayings from one of your holy books. Well, you're spot on with that one. It does when good people don't stop it.

Am not sure she heard me. She had her head stuck in a new publication. *Magical Practice in the Modern World* I think it was called. If you ask me the best use for that book is to whack some foul field around the head with it but then I'm out of touch, stuffy, too old etc so what would I know?

I do know I don't like to see people dying needlessly.

Even the Queen's Council are getting stroppy with Her Nibs over the foul fiend now. I suppose it doesn't help that many of them have had dozens of their constituents grabbed and eaten head first by that monster and the local elections are coming up soon. Politicians everywhere always keep an eye on those. Good job too. We've got to have some way of holding them to account.

I did offer my services to Her Majesty to combat the beast but again was told I was far too old. I offered to show my reflexes were still as good as they ever were but was told not to make a fuss and that the beast would soon tire of its games and head off elsewhere.

I wanted to spit blood then, I really did. Games? These aren't games. Our people are dying because Her Nibs cannot

102

face the fact she has got this wrong. The old kinds of magic still have their place in fighting evil.

The Queen told me I was far too old-fashioned. There wasn't such a thing as evil. Not these days. Not now we are all educated and know better. There are beings "with issues" and they need "patience and understanding".

I'll give that foul fiend bloody understanding all right. By the time I've finished with it, it will understand right from wrong. It will understand it is not getting away with its actions. It will understand it doesn't cross the likes of me. It will also understand it is going to die horribly if it doesn't get back to where it came from and stay there.

I have had enough. I am robing up as I dictate this into my spare wand. It's good practice in case things go wrong. It means whoever comes into my home will find it and can trace my last steps. I think you humans have something like it on planes – a black box or something.

Anyway I'm off to either be killed by the foul fiend or get sacked by my Queen for daring to tackle the beast. Hmm… I somehow think there will be a lot of bad publicity for her if she does that. Leaks to the magical press just need organising after all.

Oh yes. I know the tricks there. Some things stay evergreen in my memory, including finding methods to bring a wayward leader into line with what the rest of us just know is right.

I've studied what you humans do here and, yes, leaking bad news stories to get rid of a leader you don't want, or at the least to curb their behaviour a bit, seems like a great idea to me.

I must admit the public applause was gratifying but then my turning up in Saxbury, our capital city, all robed up in my emerald green "fighting robes" holding the head of that foul fiend aloft was bound to draw attention.

It was even better when the Queen's guards, sent out to arrest me, refused to do so and joined in with the applause. But I had the most fun I admit when I put the foul fiend's head down on the Palace steps, which Her Nibs *so* likes to waltz down, and call out very loudly, "Delivery for Her Majesty. Sign here please!"

That got a huge laugh. I expect I will pay for it tomorrow or at least once the newspaper headlines die down but I am not at all sorry.

There is only one way to deal with monsters – and that is firmly.

I must admit I didn't see that coming. Neither did Her Majesty I suspect. Or rather the *ex*-Her Majesty. The Council have shown the balls I didn't think they had (it's always nice to be wrong about something useful!).

Anyway, she's gone. Not only out of power but out of the Kingdom. Goodness knows where she's gone. Okay, I confess this isn't particularly nice of me but I hope she's gone to show some patience and understanding with that foul fiend in the next life. Well, I don't claim to be perfect.

Upshot is *I* am now Queen. Yes, you heard me. We like the monarchy here. It gives stability. But it doesn't stop my world from removing from office those who let the majesty of the monarchy down. The Council voted for me unanimously too. And my first act as Magical Sovereign Lady here?

I've created a new branch of fairy godmothers. They're older women like me but who are sharp, still have much to offer, and they are to be deployed to tackle difficult situations (so any foul fiends capable of reading this, don't say you weren't warned).

What have I called them?

Not what *she* would have done – old and makes too much of a fuss.

No. I've come up with the perfect name.

They're going to be called *The Evergreens*. We're long lasting, don't die easily, still look rather fetching in the right shade of green, and will see off any and every idiot who thinks to threaten the likes of us.

And we *will* keep going and going and going until evil vanishes for good. It's a positive aim, I think.

It should work well.

About the author

Allison Symes, who loves quirky fiction, is published by *Chapeltown Books*, *CaféLit*, and *Bridge House Publishing*.

Her flash fiction collections, *From Light to Dark and Back Again* and *Tripping the Flash Fantastic*, are available in Kindle and paperback.

She blogs on flash fiction too for a US based online magazine, *Mom's Favorite Reads*, and writes on topics of interest to writers for UK based *Chandler's Ford Today*, which is also online.

Website: https://allisonsymescollectedworks.com/

Books: http://author.to/AllisonSymesAuthorCent

YouTube:
www.youtube.com/channel/UCPCiePD4p_vWp4bz2d8oSJA/

Noel's Garden

Sheena Billett

It was only when Lucy and Adam got the tree home, Lucy realised it was too big. Adam stood to catch his breath after wrestling it into the corner where it took up around a quarter of the entire room. She'd had to move the settee over to the door to make room for it. Now it was a squeeze to get in.

"I told you it was too big!" Adam huffed in irritation.

"Well it's not your house and you don't have to live with it, little brother." Lucy punched Adam on the arm. "But thanks for helping me – I appreciate it. Time for a coffee?"

They sat, hands around cups, looking at the green giant, oddly naked and out of place in the front room of a small terraced cottage.

"Wow! Your own place and your own Christmas tree, Luce. Who'd have thought it?"

"I know. I can't believe it either. Thanks, Mum." She raised her mug in a toast, swallowing hard. "What're you going to do with your share?"

Well, I thought of travelling the world – which would have been the cool thing to do. But now I'm thinking I might use it to start my own carpentry business now I've finished the apprenticeship."

"Look at us, all grown up! Mum wouldn't have believed it."

"No…"

"It'll look better when I've decorated it," said Lucy, breaking the silence. "You don't mind me having the decs do you?" She turned to face him.

"Well, it's not as if I've got a magnificent specimen like

this to hang them on." He made a grand gesture with his arm. "But while we're on the *You don't minds*, are you sure you don't mind me going to Bel's for Christmas?"

"Adam, we've had this conversation... and no! I'll be volunteering at the homeless Christmas dinner anyway. Though I know Bel thinks all her Christmases have come at once."

Adam groaned, shaking his head. "Still got it, Luce! I think that's the cue for me to get going." He hugged her. "Have fun with the monster."

Once Lucy had got familiar decorations out of their boxes, she stood and surveyed the green canvas in front of her. Granted, she hadn't expected the tree to be so big, but she loved it – better than a penny-pinching scrawny thing cowering in the corner.

First she hung the lights – using a kitchen chair to reach the topmost branches. The top bent over where it was too tall for the ceiling, so no star or angel needed. That was okay. She took time hanging each bauble and decoration with care, savouring the memories. There was the cracked snow-scene globe Adam had thrown on the floor in temper when they'd been first allowed to decorate the tree on their own. Lucy remembered her bossy ten-year-old self with a smile. Then there were the two wooden decorations they had bought on a rare family holiday to Switzerland. She and Adam had been allowed to buy one each, which had seemed odd in the August heat. As she placed sprigs of holly, gathered surreptitiously in the woods yesterday, the light was fading.

Lucy sat with a hot chocolate as the glow of the open fire flickered over the tree in all its glory, and sighed with sorrow-tinged pleasure, breathing in the Christmas-tree smell, surrounded by warm memories of home and childhood.

107

When she turned the lights off to go to bed, she left the Christmas lights until last, marvelling at the giant, here inside her house. She had always imagined a real Christmas tree as some kind of decoration, never thinking of it as a living thing. And suddenly, she felt a sense of awe at this majestic presence in her front room.

"What on earth are you going to do with it once it drops its needles? I mean... Where are you going to get rid of it?" asked Carrie. There wasn't much room for entertaining, but Lucy had managed to squash in quite a few friends.

"Get rid of it? What do you mean?" Lucy stopped, mid-sip. She hadn't considered what would happen to the tree after Christmas, other than vague thoughts of getting Adam to take it to a tip or recycling place in his van. "It's a living thing, you don't just get rid of it!" she found herself saying.

"So what are you going to do then?"

"I'm going to plant it in the garden." Lucy made a snap decision.

"*Oh what?* It's huge! And anyway, how do you know it'll grow?"

"I don't, but I'll give it my best shot."

A few weeks later, Carrie's prediction had come to pass, and, in the heat of the room the carpet was green with needles, the fresh, piny scent replaced by something dried and dying. The tree was not looking so good.

"Time for you to get back outside where you belong, Noel," said Lucy, packing all the decorations away with care. Once she had started to think of the tree as a living thing, it had only seemed right to give it a name. Noel seemed the obvious choice.

Adam and Lucy carried Noel, still in its pot (a tree had to be gender neutral, no?) along the hall, though the kitchen,

108

and out into the chill damp of the back garden, leaving a wake of pale green behind them.

Lucy had looked up on the internet about planting out Christmas trees, and knew she needed a big hole. Once Adam had gone, she surveyed the garden, wondering where Noel would like to live. Luckily she lived in the countryside, so the garden was a reasonable size, and, not being a gardener, Lucy wasn't bothered about aesthetics; she just had some idea that she wanted her garden to be itself. Today was too cold for planting Noel – apparently it would need time to acclimatise after the heat of Christmas before it could survive putting its roots into the cold, damp earth. But she was planning to dig the hole in preparation and had bought a spade especially.

Eventually she decided in a spot in the far right-hand corner of the garden which looked fairly empty. An hour later, Lucy was sweating and breathing hard, but she reckoned the hole was the right size. She'd checked the height of the pot and dug the hole to the same depth. "What do you think of your new home, Noel?"

Noel replied by shivering its balding branches in the rising wind.

"Okay, let's get you somewhere safe, so you don't blow over." She wedged Noel in a corner by the back door and secured it in place with piles of logs.

A few days after Noel had been installed in its new home on a mild January day, the weather turned cold and snow was forecast. Being busy at work, Lucy hadn't given the weather much thought, so she was taken by surprise on a Saturday morning when she woke up to a white world. From the back bedroom she looked over the garden and gasped at Noel, resplendent in white.

"Oh my, Noel. Look at you!"

She slipped on some wellingtons and hurried out into the garden where Noel stood tall and proud. And looking down, almost camouflaged by the snow she saw several tiny clumps of snowdrops. Lucy knelt, wondering at their sudden arrival.

She took pictures on her phone and sent one to Adam.

Look at Noel in all its finery! Followed by a Christmas tree and snow flake emojis. *And snowdrops!*

Only you could have a Christmas tree with a name! came the open-mouthed reply.

The snow lasted for a week and Lucy was so proud of Noel for surviving the move and for sheltering the snowdrops from the worst of the winter weather, which had now changed to rain and a biting wind.

In March, Covid struck, and Lucy had to start working from home. She spent more time in the garden and bought a bench where she sat for her morning coffee break. At work she would have followed other people's lives on social media with a coffee on her desk, always feeling strangely drained and irritable afterwards. But things were different now – she had a garden to sit in, and it was only a few steps away. She found herself strangely refreshed when she went back to the kitchen table.

In time, she noticed something different about Noel. Some strangely-shaped leaves had appeared and… a very large purple flower. Lucy didn't know much about plants, but she did know that fir trees did not grow large purple flowers! On closer inspection, it seem that the leaves and flowers belonged to another plant that was winding its way around Noel – almost like another kind of Christmas decoration. The internet told Lucy that Noel's new friend was a clematis that flowered every spring. Lucy was thrilled to see that Noel was growing new needles on existing branches – and felt a sense of achievement at her success.

But the clematis wasn't Noel's only new friend. While drinking her morning coffee, Lucy noticed a blackbird making frequent trips in and out of the tree, flying off and returning with twigs and… something that looked like sheep's wool in its beak. The evergreen Noel was apparently providing the perfect hiding place, while other trees were yet to show off their full summer outfits. She was afraid to look too closely for fear of driving the prospective new family away. Instead, she bought some bird food and a bird table.

Morning coffee became quite a social event with blue tits, blackbirds, sparrows and other birds that Lucy didn't yet know visiting. She got used to sitting very still and just watching. Fortunately her employer didn't mind these extended morning breaks, as long as Lucy got the work done by the end of the day – which she always did.

Eventually the clematis flowers disappeared, but there was much activity from the blackbirds, who were flying to and fro, feeding their young. One afternoon while both birds were absent, Lucy crept up to Noel, who was now looking much greener, and looked. Deep inside was the nest, containing four yellow mouths. Lucy quietly stepped back and returned to her bench – overwhelmed and in awe that these blackbirds had chosen her garden to raise their family. And it was all down to Noel, who had long since outgrown its Christmas-tree phase.

When she wasn't looking, the baby blackbirds left the nest – Lucy discovered this was called "fledging". She still saw one of the young birds sitting motionless for long periods of time on the ground under the protection of Noel. She had been worried that something was wrong with it, but then suddenly it flew away. The fence was busy with sparrows coming and going from the bird table, feeding their fluttering, demanding, young. How had she never noticed all this spring-time activity before?

Soon Noel began to be overshadowed by the large oak tree and several sycamores along the hedge at the bottom of the garden. Lucy had now acquired a selection of books about trees, birds and plants, and found herself making notes about the living things that made her garden home, as well as those who paid fleeting visits, like long-lost relatives or adult children. For the first time, Noel was looking rather insignificant, dwarfed by giants even more majestic, but seemingly content to move out of the lime-light for a season.

Lock-down life had a quiet and calmness about it – something Lucy had never experienced before. She'd always thought of herself as a sociable person, and if there were any parties, she was always up for them. "I'm worried," said Carrie once garden visits were allowed and Lucy had waxed lyrical about Noel, the blackbird family, and her garden social life. "I'm worried that you're turning into a batty old cat lady, at twenty-five."

"But I don't have a cat."

"You know what I mean!" Carrie put her cup down on the seat between them. "The first chance we've had to go out on the town – well out to a pub anyway, in ages, and you're not buzzing. In fact you don't even seem that bothered about coming, which I take as a personal affront." She place her hand on her chest dramatically. "Don't get all boring and preachy about the environment on us, Lucy."

On reflection, Lucy realised that Carrie was right – she had changed. She wasn't looking forward to the night out, but she'd agreed to go in the end because she didn't want to lose her friends. And maybe it was important to get back to some sort of normality and have a social life with actual people, rather than with the trees, plants and birds in her garden.

The noise in the canvas tent in the pub garden was deafening. The thud of the music and over-excited screaming and shouting made it hard to think, never mind actually talk to anyone. How had she not noticed all this noise before? The best bit about a night out had always been getting drunk to the stage where nothing really mattered any more, other than having a good time. Lucy downed several shots with Carrie – playing their customary drinking game, but it just wasn't the same; there wasn't that thrill of feeling the alcohol kicking in and the prospect of some kind of temporary oblivion. Lucy realised that she no longer wanted to lose control, to blot everything out. How pointless it all seemed, *and* the wasted next day battling a hangover. The living things in her garden didn't need to get drunk, they were too focussed on living and regenerating – the important things in life. They didn't have the luxury of time to fritter away. She felt the oppressive heat, trapped under the canvas, overwhelming her, and she had to escape. She told Carrie she wasn't feeling well and was going outside to wait for a taxi home. Carrie was well gone by this stage and simply slurred, "You're such a drag, Lucy," before turning back to the man she'd hooked up with.

Outside, the summer evening stillness was more powerful than any alcohol-induced excitement. As Lucy stood, as well as the distant thud of the music, she picked up the sound of an owl. She was motionless, revelling in the still evening air, when from nowhere the owl appeared and perched on a fence post across the road. Lucy hardly dared to breathe as it regarded her with beady eyes, illuminated in the moonlight that flooded the scene as the clouds parted. They shared a wordless minute before it swivelled its head, looking away from her. And then, as suddenly as it had appeared it flew off into the night as the clouds closed their curtains, blocking out the light. The two-minute show was over and Lucy allowed herself to breathe again, wondering at her fortune that this creature of the wild had chosen to engage with her.

In July, Adam was killed. A blow-out on the motorway.

Time stopped and Lucy spoke to no one. She didn't turn on her phone or lap-top for a week. She spent time in the garden, watching the clouds cross the sky, and the butterflies and bees busy working the various flowers that had appeared from nowhere. And on the day it rained she sat on the bench under an umbrella until she was numb from the damp, chill air of the wet summer's day.

A persistent ringing of the doorbell, eventually drew her back to the dark reality that she could no longer escape. "Lucy, where have you been? I've been trying to get you!" said Bel, her arms folded angrily across her chest.

"Sorry… I… I'm so sorry. Come in." She stood aside to make room for Bel to pass in the narrow hall-way, noticing the greasy, tangled hair and creased sundress as Bel headed for the kitchen. Lucy felt a wash of pity and shame flow over her. Why hadn't she thought to see how Bel was? Why hadn't she understood that she was the one person that Bel could have talked to about Adam?

"This isn't just about you, Lucy! You're not the only one suffering." Bel burst into tears, and as she held her. Lucy found, at last, her own tears. She didn't know how long they held each other and cried.

"You know, I've always been a little bit jealous of you." Bel tucked a strand of hair behind her ear. They were sitting at the kitchen table having toasted Adam with their wine. "Adam was always talking about you."

"Really?" Lucy found it hard to imagine Adam talking very much about anything, least of all her.

"He told me all about your Christmas tree. Did you really give it a name?"

"Yup. I'm afraid so."

"He always looked up to you, you know. Maybe it's because your mum died and your dad is, well…"

"You can say it. He's in prison,"

Bel dropped her gaze to the table. "I'm sorry… I didn't mean to… but Adam would never talk about it."

"He's in prison for fraud. Lots of pensioners lost their savings because of him. Apparently he's got Alzheimer's now and doesn't know what's what anymore, so he might as well be dead really." Uncomfortable about how callous that had sounded, Lucy refilled their glasses. "So Adam and I only had each other. And now it's just me."

"Well… maybe not, actually."

Lucy narrowed her eyes. "What do you mean?"

"I'm pregnant."

Lucy looked out of the window, and then back at Bel. "Really?"

"You'll be an aunty… So it's not just you."

Lucy needed time to get her head around this news, and so abruptly changed the subject. "How would you like to come and meet Noel in person?"

"You're joking, right?"

"Come this way."

They stood in the dappled, late-afternoon shade, as Noel waved its branches at them in the breeze. Examining Noel's newly-produced cones, Bel said, "Wow, when you look at these up close, they are amazing! Look at all these patterns and shapes. I bet I could draw one of these."

The following day, Bel reappeared with a sketch pad and some pencils. After a few hours of impatiently turning

115

pages and rubbing out, she showed Lucy a stunning set of sketches of Noel's cones, seen from various angles, and with different tones of light and shade. "Where did you learn to draw like that? Adam never said anything about you being an artist."

"I'm not. And I haven't done anything since I did A-level art. But then, I guess I thought I should get a proper job that would earn actual money, so I started waitressing and I met Adam and... that was that."

"But you're on furlough now, and you've got time on your hands. And you're good, so..." Lucy cocked her head to one side.

In the end, Bel spent so much time at Lucy's that she began to stay over, and before they knew it, she had moved in. Together they, without realising it, embarked on a project to record every living thing in Lucy's garden. Bel photographed and then drew and painted, capturing the beauty of even the smallest ant, while Lucy found out the names of everything from the internet and her increasing library of nature books, and wrote about them – where they were found and the dates. Bel and Lucy knew, without having to say it, that this was their way of surviving.

They spent many hours talking about Adam, each discovering a side of him that they hadn't known, and the days passed in a suspended, peaceful stillness. There were times of tears, times of silence, and, increasingly, times of laughter – often at Adam's expense.

Eventually, Bel went back to work part-time. Her employer was apologetic about it, but Bel told him not to worry, as her parents were helping her out until things improved.

"We should give this thing we're doing a name," said Bel one evening, hands protective over her growing bump in the first chill of autumn. Lucy had spent the afternoon collating and organising everything they had produced so far, and there was a surprising amount of it.

"*Noel's Garden*. That's what we should call it. Maybe make it into a book for children... and we'll dedicate it to Autumn, said Lucy sitting up, indicating Bel's stomach.

"I told you, she's not going to be called Autumn, Lucy!"

"Okay, well it'll do for now, as that's roughly when she'll be born. Anyway... what do you think about *Noel's Garden?*"

Over the next few weeks as the showy colours of autumn receded, Noel took on a starring role, once again – its dark-green looking lush and verdant against the browns and blacks of the dying trees and summer plants. Fungi appeared beneath its branches overnight, alien but strangely captivating beings, existing in full sight for only a few days before disappearing back into oblivion.

Autumn arrived, several weeks before Christmas, weighing in at seven pounds, and disturbing the peace of the cottage. Her attention captured by the magic and wonder of the new arrival, and with the accompanying fatigue of sleepless nights, Lucy hadn't thought about a Christmas tree, or even decorations until, suddenly, it was the week before Christmas.

She did what felt right, and bought a set of outdoor lights and decorations. And while Bel and Autumn were having a nap, she decorated Noel for the second time. This time, you'll be the star where you belong, outside," she said, standing back to admire her handiwork. Noel twinkled back at her in the dusk. The indoor decs would keep for another year when Autumn would be old enough to admire them.

Sitting in camp chairs, with rugs, hot chocolate and marshmallows, Lucy, Bel, Bel's parents and Autumn in her carry chair admired Noel in silence. Lucy remembered last Christmas and looked around fondly at her new family. "You did good, Adam," she whispered.

The following year, *Noel's Garden* appeared in the village bookshop, and thanks to a marketing campaign by Bel's father, who turned out to be a wizard at publicity, Noel soon had its own Facebook, Instagram and Tik-Tok pages. At Lucy's insistence, they had stretched the truth to include a barn owl.

After several weeks of plucking up the courage and getting past the Covid-related red tape, Lucy went to visit her father. Somehow she had expected him to still look the same – an older version of Adam, but here was a frail, vulnerable old man, who didn't know who she was. Even so, she told him about Adam, and was surprised at the tears gathering in his eyes. She held his hand and sat with him for a while. He died the following week.

Bel decided to enrol in art school, and Aunty Lucy did child-minding duties, between school visits and library story-telling sessions. And thanks to Noel, a new generation of children – and quite a few adults – learned about the miracle of nature, the wonder of the living things on their doorsteps, and the evergreen cycle of life. When the full collection of notes and drawings was eventually published as, *A Year in Noel's Garden,* and dedicated to Adam, a new life opened its doors for Lucy and Bel.

About the author
Sheena has always been an avid reader of anything and everything, and is a firm believer that you can never have too many books. Although she loved her previous career as a music teacher, she is now loving life as a fiction editor and, lately, a writer. The everyday has always fascinated Sheena and much of her writing is based on snippets of conversations overheard in

cafés, shops or anywhere that people are together. She aims for writing that is a blend of observational humour (think Victoria Wood or Peter Kaye) and emotionally challenging situations for her characters to deal with, all within the context of a good story. There is always a What if? question to be answered in a her stories. In Noel's Garden, the question is: What if someone realises that their Christmas tree is a living thing and something much more than just an indoor decoration for a few weeks?

If you would like to read more tales like this, *Shifting Horizons*, Sheena's first book of short stories, is available on most online platforms. Her newest book, *From Manchester to the Arctic*, comes out in January 2023. It is set in 1970s Canadian Arctic and is about a young newly qualified nurse from Manchester who answers a newspaper ad: "Wanted: Nurses with a sense of adventure." Find out more at https://sheenabillettauthor.com

Norway Spruce

James Ward

I write this from cell block E. This is my third passing through prison. It will be my last. I will not get out this time. What pains the most is the knowledge that this third and fatal trip to the kingdom of concrete walls could have been so easily avoided – if only I hadn't already been here, if only this wasn't my third.

I have spent most of my life either unhappy or caged; there was one festive period, the rain and snow of the last year gone by, in which I was neither. I liked the taste of normalcy I briefly enjoyed, though, by nature, all taste – no matter how sweet – is temporary.

My first sentence was passed after I tried to rob a bank with my older brother and two of his friends. We lived in a village about twenty minutes' drive from Macclesfield. One Saturday, after no planning and a violently drunk evening in the Golden Crow the night previous, we heartily stormed into a bank, (I don't remember which one – it was long ago, I was still drunk from our fun in the Crow) all wearing masks of outdated Halloween references and with Tony's – my brother's friend – selection of shotguns held in our sweaty hands.

I can't speak for the other lads but under the thick, glass-proof gloves my hands itched from the inside as bugs trapped under a carpet, dripping anxiety poured from every possible escape. Tony was fine, or at least he looked it, after all they were his shotguns from his farm so why wouldn't he be comfortable pointing them at the pregnant lady behind the counter?

My brother had talked a huge game (he always did) but when I chanced a peak over my shoulder to check on him,

I saw a cowering boy in way over his head, staring back at me, I saw myself, and in all our shared years we had not once looked alike. Mark was blonde where I was brown, thin in the places I was fat, smart where I was foolish. Until now. Now we were completely akin, hidden by the same broken Scream mask and separated only by shaking bodies on the floor, hands over their heads and thoughts with God.

Not a single shot was fired. The police waited patiently as we strolled out onto Roe Street with £20,000 in our drawstring bags. Five each. Although I had never seen that much money in my short lifetime, it was no more than a pitiful steal; all our shares pooled together wouldn't have been enough to keep Tony's farm afloat and, in the end, of course, we saw none of it. We were thrown into our bolted chambers on the Saturday night and by the Monday afternoon, all the cows and chickens had been moved to a new field, a new home.

I didn't see any of those boys, least my brother, for a while after but I was never bothered by anything like that. The second of my brother's friends – the first to drop his JD bag and throw his hands to the sky when he saw the flashing blue and fluorescent yellow – cried all through the long night in the cell opposite to mine. He didn't just cry, he wept and begged and banged his head against the metal door to the point where I veritably hoped to forget his name. Mission accomplished, yet his face has never left; even veiled by the mask, I remember his spotty cheeks, skin that was red and always burning, stringy, chapped lips which held the weight of an unignorably abject cleft lip above, all placed on a fairly round head and face. His was Freddy Kreuger.

It was my brother himself who taught me not to miss or pine for people so he couldn't be too offended by my flippancy to his removal from my life. "Crying over folks you've lost is for women," he would remind me whenever I got just a little sentimental about the five-minute mates I had made and lost over my stunted – at that time, I'm old as China now – history. Perhaps my brother was a terrible influence, yes; as I look back, there is no arguing the fact. But I still managed to throw my life away without his being there, and as such, I'm not sure how much blame can really be put on Mark. Believe me, I've been trying to place all of it in his ungrateful lap since my second trip to what is now and forever my home.

I will not describe at length the events that caused me to spend a meaty chunk of my existence trapped by bars, only that I was desperate, and I never wanted anyone to get hurt. I was married by that point to a woman, originally from Iran, who had left her husband for me and resented me for doing so when she realised the person I truly was. We were without a coin, vain and addicted and all those who have known the warm hug of addiction also know the cold stare of dependency when whatever it is the weakling so craves cannot be hunted or gathered.

It was another Saturday night, this one sleeting cold with wild winds, when I drove down to Tony's farm – now some other family's castle. No matter, most of the guns were kept in the same shed. I aimed smaller: this time not a bank with three other fools but a lone petrol station where I would try my hand by oneself.

Like I said, I do not wish to divulge to you the gruesome happenings of that night. I want to tell you about my time with the Hullums. I will vouch that I am not and have never been any kind of racist, despite what the newspapers, the judge, and the victim's family might have said. I did not kill him because he was Indian. I killed him because if I didn't pull the trigger, he would have overpowered me, taken the shotgun predominantly used for ending pesky vermin such as foxes and rabbits, and done just that; it would have been me dead on the freshly mopped floor, not him, and naturally, I didn't want that. So I shot him through the chest and took the £358 he had in his register. Understand – I was poor, hooked and married; I had nothing to live for and yet, in the most human way, I wished to live on anyway.

And live on I did, another twenty years spent and still I got off lightly. I shouldn't have had the opportunity to spend a Christmas outside of cell block E, (or was I up in C?) but I did. I was eighteen when I fell to my knees on Roe Street. I walked out this second time a forty-one-year-old with no plan and no idea where my brother was.

About two years before I was released, I had recognised an old friend in the canteen. An old friend: more like a fellow resident of the village, which in the outside world, or in this case, the inside world, constituted as a brother in blood and bondage. We ate jacket potatoes next to each other and played chess as we talked about people and memories from the village, laughing at our backwardness and scorning anyone who didn't rigorously follow our troubled ways.

As he took my bishop one day, effectively ending the game, he asked me if I ever received any visitors. I told him I didn't. He informed me that Rupert Hullum, another mascot, was managing to come in and see him from time to time. Rupert was something close to a genuine old friend; we had been pally in high school, playing on the rugby and cricket team together, me an outside centre and spin bowler, him a scrumhalf and top of the order. He had always showed me kindness, though he was from a very different background to me – something Mark had always detested Rupert and, at times, me for. But Mark had been dead for eight years, I just didn't know it yet; and even if I had known, it wouldn't have changed my decision to see Rupert at the next available visitation day, if, that is, Rupert wanted to see me.

His family lived at the top of the hill, but the boy never used it to look down on the people, I think that's the best way to describe him: shy and politely embarrassed by his family's extreme (compared to the other villagers) wealth. I referred to him as a boy just now, but by the time I saw him on visitation day, he was customarily a man, though he still looked the same: short, with small but very blue eyes, fair hair in length and colour and workman hands that stuck out like mushroom clouds over an explosion from his sleeves. The only thing that had changed was he now sported a hearty moustache – which I thought gave him a rather presidential look – and he was rounded out at the middle. I had spent the better part of two decades living off cold but surprisingly pleasant dollops of swede thus losing my healthy country-boy figure.

We laughed at how we had changed, upon which the conversation turned quiet as we realised that boys from where we're from never really change. Each second Saturday of the month followed this pattern until one day Rupert noticed I wasn't my usual self; I think the novelty of having a friend was starting to wear off and I was doing what I usually did when I got comfortable: regressing in floods of self-sabotage and isolation. I think he was worried that I might kill myself as the little I did speak was grave and depressed. Alas, if my run in with the petrol shop clerk didn't lead you to infer, I'm most afraid of death so suicide was never an option.

He offered me some seasonal work on his farm when (and if) I finally got out and then he left. I didn't see him again until I marched, wearing the old football top I had worn the day I was arrested, up the largest hill in the village on a bitter evening – I forget the day itself – towards the

Hullum's family home and business. There's was a farm but not like old Tony's, it did not harvest livestock or grow wheat: it was a Christmas tree farm.

I remember thinking how gorgeous and oddly shaped the house was as I knocked on the great wooden door with one of those handles that's like a lion's mouth with a semi-circular bar clenched in its jaw. Marianne screamed when she opened the door and saw a sodden stranger wiping his boots on the welcome mat which read "The Hullums Welcome You!". I can't, nor don't, blame her, I must have looked a monster. I explained that I was here to see Rupert and apologised for scaring her. Then the man who had lit up every second Saturday of the month at 1 pm with his broad and welcoming smile frowned concernedly at me, not letting me in, rubbing his brow and saying "Right" repeatedly when I told him I was here to take him up on his most generous offer.

"Do you have anywhere to stay?"

I didn't.

"Right…"

He spoke to his family, who were sat at the dinner table just out of view from the front door, enjoying a warm spaghetti Bolognese, only a vegetarian version as Marianne, Rupert's girlfriend, I later learned, didn't eat meat. This was to be the first of many hushed but charged conversations about me; most of which situated me in the next adjoining room or, in this case, on the other side of a door, hearing snippets of harried conversation, mainly Marianne's shrill voice. "What do you owe him?" "You've always been like this: a complete pushover." "A prisoner?"

It occurred to me that I had never told Rupert the reason behind my time in the box. He had never asked. If it was because he already knew then he did me the courtesy of never telling his family who certainly wouldn't have much approved, much less let me stay and work alongside them; especially Marianne, a constant activist and defender of those lost rights in the far east, whose hatred for me started when I knocked on the homely wooden door, long before she found out the reason for my being there.

After I stood in the rain a little longer, Rupert opened the door once again and informed me that I could stay at the farm and work – such happy news told with such a sombre face. He said the log cabin "wasn't quite ready" by which he meant: there was still lots of expensive stuff I could steal under cover of darkness, so I stayed in the garage for a couple of nights. It may seem that the Hullums treated me somewhat harshly but in truth, it was the most kindness I had ever been shown.

Due to Jarvis, patriarch of the family, the business, and the family business, going on the national news the year previous, the farm was due to have its busiest season to date and was set up to open up shop two weeks earlier than usual. That suited me perfectly, arriving in early November.

The work was numbing and honest, the only sincere job I'd ever had. My life had been a clear pattern of tending bars or encased by them. I could finally breathe real air again; up so high I could reach up and swipe through the racing clouds of frost.

Foremostly, I worked with a man named Frank who Jarvis liked to remind the group was a "Thieven' drunk and an alco". Which seemed unfair to me, given that the leader himself was never, as he called it, "In the field" without his trusty hipflask filled to the brim with festive rum. Everyone else in the regiment who wasn't a Hullum held lowly attributes and were good friends of the thieving and the drinking. This has always led me to wondering why he picked on the old man more than the others, me for instance.

I ate breakfast with Frank every morning in the main cabin of the farm where everything was wooden, the reception desk decorated with small potted trees and a fire that never stopped burning in the corner. Me and Frank would eat bread rolls by the coffee machine without saying a word to one another. Our bauble red hats sat on the table, shaking slightly as our table wobbled under the weight of Frank's massive arms, with one of the six Christmas songs that played on repeat humming faintly from behind us.

He had a nose the shape and colour of a plum only much larger, and we both knew the other was in some way troubled, followed by a past that had chased and cornered them up a snowy mountain.

The only time we did speak was to communicate names of families and coordinates of trees. Our labour was simple enough: Molly, the receptionist who looked down and cleaned her glasses whenever I entered the cabin, would hand me or the drunk a checkboard with a series of family's names next to their corresponding tree followed by the place to find it in the continuous rows of pine. Four fields, the tallest and greenest in Field 1 by the main cabin, each with chains of trees labelled all the way to "ZZZZ", one hundred trees to a chain. Our record was a checkboard (that was two sheets of ten to twelve trees) in an hour, but you needed The Gator to hit those times. Once you find the tree, tagged with a yellow piece of plastic similar to the ones I saw on the ears of the pigs at Tony's farm, it was then cut at the bottom with a small chainsaw – though I was never allowed to hold the instrument – carefully slid it into a wheelbarrow – root at your end so you can see over the beast – and taken down to netting. All the chainsaws and netting machines had names of their own, Frank's was called Horacio for some reason, and he talked to the blade more than he looked at me. There was Sandra, the big red netter, (only for the most boastful trees and families) and Stevie, the much more used and liked netter, at the top of Field 2, which, if one was driving or sliding around in the back of The Gator was a three-minute drive through mud and snow from any point in the farm, but if you found yourself with a thirty kilo tree sat in your pigeon-hearted wheelbarrow in the far reaches of Field 4, it was a question of endurance and sheer stomach, the kind of work prison taught you to long for when sat alone in cell block E. When arrived at Sandra or Stevie, or the two situated right next to the main hut for the families who liked to watch the quick and boring process, (for a little extra) named Turner and Berry, you would slide the tree, always root first, into what resembled a reversed cement mixer with holes at both ends and a net over and inside it. Next would be to pull the tree out the other side and cut the excess net with cutters which also had dreadful names but thankfully they have now become a mystery, tie a knot at each end and collect the additional five pounds from the family.

That process was repeated endlessly for a month and a half, all spoken in codes between me and Frank: "Scotch Pine. 4, SS12. McAdam's, Tues, Del." "White Pine. 1, C65. Tracy & Kat, Mon, Coll." "Grand Fir. 4, UUU57. Johnson, Fri, Del."

The first tree in which I completed the whole process individually, save the cutting of the tree, was a Norway Spruce. Field 4, LL32. Adam Clever, Monday, delivery. I hope he enjoyed his tree and his Christmas.

Frank did talk once on what was to be his last day. Drunk as the way they found him, he stumbled into cabin as I stirred my tea (I've always despised the smell of coffee) and told me that he used to own a chainsaw shop of his very own, that he was afraid of needles and that his mother was in a home of sorts. Then he walked out of the cabin, past

128

Jarvis who hurled hurtful northern words and muddy snow at him from the decking, and out of the farm. He didn't come back.

Thereupon I was partnered with Phil, a lad of the age I was before my first visit. A local kid who didn't like wearing the red company hat, so he brought his own, woolly and handmade. He was soon to become my only friend at the farm. Rupert had started to work more on the delivery side of the operation and that didn't trouble me, his habit of avoiding conversation with me grew as the snow-filled days passed, and I caught his girlfriend, who did not work, watching me from the kitchen window more than once, a couple of times not having the decency or embarrassment to look away.

As the days of Christmas (for it is not one day) approached, I was asked to join him for a drink once or twice and then an agreement was made that not a white moon would pass without mine and Phil's bottles being raised to it. There was nothing to do; we weren't just in the middle of nowhere, we were on the edge of it, untouched by city light we drank and looked at the trees, sharing little of ourselves but certainly venturing further than me and old Frank ever managed. Phil was allowed in the house, and he stole me cookies that Marianne had baked for the family.

I have a lot of regret, but only two instances with Phil come to mind as ending sourly: the first being the rabbits. All farms, even ones that grow Christmas trees, keep the guns in the same place. What's worse is Jarvis actively encouraged the "Cleansing" as he so festively put it. I pitied what he called pests and only after three nights of bangs and high-pitched squeals did I decide to leave that job to Phil, and get back to my drinking. The second had slightly weightier ramifications. After a particularly hard day, where a fourteen-foot Douglas Fir snapped and toppled in the wind consequently rolling down the hill this yuletide empire sat on, crushing a large chunk of Field 2 and a poorly parked Mini Cooper in its path, me and the youngster decided to hop in The Gator.

Phil had a car but was far too drunk to drive and the shop that was always ten minutes from closing was only five minutes away. With the hope and aim of being there and back before anyone had noticed what had happened, we jumped in the green beast. The Gator was a standard all-terrain farm vehicle that had the heart of a tank and the speed of a reptile in water; one of the back left wheels would constantly lock up but after some words of encouragement and a purposeful but steady kick, she would always see things our way.

We had no time for such amendments when speeding out of the main entrance, sliding through the icy mud, taking the handmade sign that dazzled over the trees down with us, not forgetting about a dozen trees. The whole family came out, even Marianne and the mother, who I never saw apart from that first day on the rain-soaked Hullum porch, her worried stare creeping through the gap in the door to paradise. Even Molly was there, her glasses firmly on her head.

Rupert said nothing but Jarvis had taken the last sip from his flask. I'd chiefly thought him to be a brash but unthreatening man, stubby in size and menacing only in rank – but this wasn't business, it was family Christmas time. Woe was Jarvis, pacing and babbling; he knew he couldn't fire the drunken pair that stood cowering by their wreck like scolded mutts that fouled their homes; we were both homeless. Phil slept in his car, but I don't think he wanted anyone to know, in-keeping with the tradition of the place and the people who lived there but didn't call it home. It was a week until Christmas and Jarvis had nobody else, there was nobody else, they had all walked. So he took my finger.

I couldn't repay him for The Gator, or the trees, or the sign, and I couldn't give him the satisfaction of firing me, so he took my little finger on my left hand with Bonnie, his saw named after an infamous French executioner. He then threw it to his dog, a horrible thing that looked like a ragged teddy bear, who fed gladly upon it.

Some of the family screamed – not Marianne – and led me inside the house where I looked at family pictures on the wall, holidays, weddings, graduations as Molly bandaged up my hand, muttering to herself and making sure her glasses didn't tip off her nose; the family had the last of their mumbled meetings with the mother watching me listen through the crack in the wood.

Not much was said between then and Christmas day. I worked, Phil worked, we spoke in coordinates just as me and the man before him had done, I forget his name. My brother's friend, the crier, stopped by the farm to pick up a tree for his family. Fraser Fir. 1, RRR 83. My Brother's Friend, Sat, Coll. He told me that my brother had been killed in prison many years ago, then tipped me a tenner.

The day eventually arrived. I was admiring the empty fields and the thousands of stumps that would grow alpine and fat before Jarvis and the Hullums were through with them when Rupert tapped me on my shoulder and with a few stutters, like he was talking to a stranger, invited me to Christmas dinner with the family.

I gratefully accepted and enjoyed what must be, looking back, the best meal I have ever enjoyed. I was accepted into the warm hug that was their family life for an evening of stuffing, wine and people on the TV in the background with cracker hats falling off their head. Everyone was warm and we ate until our plates were stricken of any evidence that there ever was a bounty to be eaten. Marianne couldn't resist the turkey or the chicken and Molly looked me dead in the eye when she told me about the gifts she'd received from her fiancé: Tim, an engineer of a kind, who seemed to me, when all the family's eye pointed down, another unfortunate stowaway of the Hullums, not fit for Field 1.

After it was all finished, Rupert passed me a thousand pounds in cash, I hadn't remembered to ask to be paid, and then he told me I couldn't stay any longer. Not that he hated me, the festive period was simply coming to an end. He told me about his father's bouncy castle business that they cowboyed in the summer and how, if I wished, I could come back and join the team again. I accepted the offer knowing I had no intention of blowing up bouncy castles in the summer, shook his hand and was gone by Boxing Day morning.

The money lasted a bit. I robbed again when it was gone, nobody died this time. I wasn't against the idea of a return visit; nowhere – not even the Hullum's – was home save this place of misery and containment. I sit in cell block E, thinking of the immortal line of trees that marched along Field 4 and how long it had taken to grow, after all, they started planting in 2006.

About the author
James is an actor as well as a writer. His debut was in *Nobody Loves You & You Don't Deserve to Exist*, screened in multiple venues in Manchester and now available on Amazon Prime. He wrote and directed *Me & Thee* in April 2022 at The Empty Space Theatre, and has recently started his masters in creative writing at The University of Salford.

Shelf Life

Clair Humphries

It's Fridays I like best. They're the noisiest days, thanks to all the little ones, but don't tell Joan because they drive her mad.

"Not those tambourines again," she says, wincing; Toddler Time always gives her one of her heads. Then she goes outside for a ciggie while I read the telly pages and listen to *The Wheels On The Bus*. I'm good at listening and Joan's good at talking, which is why we get on. I met her on a Monday, when the library was running its Silver Surfer drop-ins before they had all the cuts. I've not touched the computer in years – that was Frank's baby, really – but it was free and I thought why not? There's only *Homes Under the Hammer* at that time in the morning, so it was an excuse to get out of the flat. They put Joan next to me and straight away she was off, telling me all about her daughter in Dubai. She'd sent an iPad over so they could Facetime, but Joan was scared to open the box. We didn't stay long; apparently week four was Tablets and it was only week one which was Optimizing Google, so Joan said she'd sit that one out. The librarian was nice, though.

"What are you ladies searching for?" she asked when she came round. I said some drama on a Saturday night would be good, instead of the usual talent show rubbish and Joan said was there any chance of a cup of tea? The librarian said our luck was in; apparently they'd just turned the Reference section into a Chillout Zone, so we found a sofa by the vending machine and settled down.

Joan and I don't agree on everything – I read the *Mirror*, she likes the *Daily Mail* – but we rub along. One thing we do have in common is our love of cakes; that's our secret, come tea-time. Joan always sneaks out, just before eleven, to pop into Greggs next door. I put our usual papers to one side and find a nice big one like the *Telegraph,* then we hunker down behind it with a sticky bun. The staff never catch us but if they did Joan would give them what for – never mind all the snotty signs about No Eating On The Premises. You can get ten types of coffee from the machine so it's fine to chill out with a hot drink but eating cake's a crime! Anyway, as Joan says, it's harmless fun and it breaks the day because we usually stay until twelve. Then I like to get home for *Loose Women* before lunch.

Every Tuesday they have Book Club – not that Joan approves.
   "A library's no place for books," she always says loudly when the group come in and I must say the council seems to agree. Half the shelves are empty these days, which is a shame; the staff must be too busy optimising search engines to put any books out. Then again, what do I know? "I've survived seventy-nine years without reading a book," Joan likes to remind me. "Never did my Linda any harm, either." I can't argue with that; I've seen the photos of her daughter's swimming pool on the phone she sent her last Christmas. Linda married well – her husband runs some big multinational firm or other – and she worked her way up from Filing to Office Manager and then became his PA. Joan says he always held a torch for her and it came to a head at one Christmas do, when Linda was handing round the canapes and he said he was leaving his wife. That was thirty years ago and they've never been happier, plus they're mortgage-free and living it up in the sun. I think he has a bit of a controlling streak – Linda rings up sometimes, complaining – but Joan always puts her straight. You can't have everything in life, can you? And besides, he pays for her personal trainer and

hairdresser and nail technician, so she's got no excuse to let herself go. Joan's hoping the family might come over for her eightieth birthday next month, with her new great-granddaughter, Gracie. She's just waiting for the text to confirm.

Joan's favourite day is Wednesday. It's Arts and Crafts at ten-thirty, with biscuits thrown in. I usually leave her to it – Frank was into his woodwork and painting and so on – but I'm all fingers and thumbs. I struggle to thread a needle if I'm honest, unlike Joan. She's working on a rag doll for Gracie and it's going really well.

"You've dressed that doll lovely, Joan," I said to her last time she showed me.

"Gorgeous, isn't it?" she said, running a hand over its sparkly dress and fluffy pink boots. "Linda said our Gracie loves a bit of bling – she's got a pair of diamanté studded baby Uggs on order for her first birthday – so I reckon she'll love this."

"Course she will, Joan," I said warmly, although I must admit to having reservations about the sequins. It seemed a bit of a choking hazard for the little one, but I didn't like to say. Why shouldn't Joan enjoy spoiling her family? Frank and I never had children – not that it mattered, not really. We didn't need anyone else; we were together, a team. Obviously, we had our moments but I don't like to dwell because what's the point? There was that winter – whatever year it was, with all the power cuts and we spent most evenings in one room, trying to keep warm. It all blurs into one now. Anyway, it was the fourth time it happened and I remember Frank shouting at the doctor – not that it was his fault and not that Frank had a temper but we'd both just had enough – and that was that. It was fine; the next year rolled around and there was a lovely hot summer and life carried on. Not like these days, with everyone telling the world their business. I never could stand *Tricia* or *Jeremy Kyle*.

Thursday is Housebound day.

"Would you like to go on our list, ladies? Save your legs?" the librarian asked once and Joan went mad.

"There's nothing wrong with my legs! Damn cheek..." She'd just had her roots done and was wearing a lovely new top from M&S, so I could see her point. Joan used to work in Ladieswear and she knows what's what. She's offered to give me a makeover but I said no. I can't stand all that fussing about. Sometimes I have to put my foot down, even though it's not in my nature, because she can be too forceful for her own good. Of course, she's had to be tough, what with her Len carrying on, but not everyone understands. I do. I've seen all sorts: the scars up her arm, the faint white marks where he ripped her earrings clean out. It's a shame, when she rubs people up the wrong way, especially the librarians because they're always looking out for us and they only want to help. Like their housebound service, not that I'd give in to that. I've always made an effort to get out of the flat. Even after—

No. I don't want to think about that. I don't need to think about it most of the time, not when the telly's on, filling his space. All I'll say is that it's too quiet indoors. Better to be in here, listening. To Joan and all the little ones and their mums and dads singing along.

"Have they done *Twinkle, Twinkle* yet?" Joan returns and sits down, squashing me into a corner of the sofa. I fold my paper up and pass her today's *Mail*.

"Just finishing now," I say, watching as the parents start loading up their buggies. The librarian walks over, looking harassed. "Busy one today?" I ask with a sympathetic smile.

"Packed," she says. "And there's only me now we've lost

136

our volunteers. Karen's on jury service and Bernard's joined Men in Sheds at the community centre on Fridays – he said he misses working with his hands. He's making us a new DVD returns box, which is nice, but I could do with his hands here if I'm honest. It's wearing me out, juggling the shakers and the tambourines, and no-one else is keen…"

"That's a shame," I say. "You'd think people would want—" And then Joan's phone starts buzzing and she jumps up, all flushed.

"Ooh, this is it! Just popping out before the phone police get their knickers in a twist." She glares at the librarian and rushes off, pushing her way through the buggies by the sliding doors.

"It's her Linda," I tell the librarian and then I hear my voice say: "I'm happy to volunteer. I mean, if I'm not too old…" which is strange because I don't usually pipe up.

"Oh, that would be great!" the librarian beams at me. "You know it can get a bit noisy—"

"I don't mind the noise. It would do me a favour, actually, because there's nothing much on Fridays before *Bargain Hunt* and that doesn't start till four…" Then I see Joan coming back and the librarian says something about risk assessments and checks and forms but for once I'm only half-listening. Joan stands there, completely still, and we look at each other for a moment before the librarian wanders off.

"Busy?" I say and she nods.

"Some corporate do he's hosting. My Linda needs to be there, sorting out nibbles and whatnot," she shrugs, waving her arm. "It's not her fault—"

"No."

"She works all hours, you know. She's a good girl."

"I know."

"Maybe next year. For my eighty-first. I'll make another

doll for Gracie, a matching pair. And it's just a birthday – no big deal..."

"At our age? Of course, it's a big deal. Get yourself over here," I say, patting the sofa and for once Joan does what she's told. "Now then. How about you find us a nice big paper and I'll nip next door for a proper cake? I fancy something really gooey today, with fresh cream and jam—"

"I'll go," she says and I raise my hand without thinking. She flinches.

"Sorry," I say. "Look, you're staying here. It's my turn now." Then I make my way to the doors, treading lightly between the buggies and smiling at the little ones; they look so content in there, all safe and wrapped up. It'll be nice to join them, even if it is just once a week, for a bit of a sing-song and anyway, what have I got to lose?

It's about time I tried something new.

About the author

Clair Humphries is a freelance writer and Content Partner for Ordnance Survey. She was a finalist in the Jane Austen Short Story Award and BBC Laughing Stock and her stories have appeared in a range of magazines and anthologies. Clair has a keen interest in social history and writes regular features for local magazine *Dartford Living*. She has also written for *Black and Green* magazine, *Henpicked.com* and *CultureTrip.com* amongst others. She is at her happiest in a library, eavesdropping on conversations, which was where the inspiration for *Shelf Life* came about...

www.clairhumphries.com

The Evergreens

Jeanne Davies

Mr and Mrs Green are going to be celebrating their wedding anniversary after fifty years of happiness. That's what the invitation said.

Their daughter, Chloe, examined the elaborate card carefully, scrutinising the undertones of the wording. She couldn't believe her mother had organised a big party when her father was enduring the late stages of heart failure. The last time she saw him he looked as pale as a ghost, frail, weak and barely able to walk. How could she put him through this Chloe wondered, especially as he'd never been a fan of social occasions. She immediately telephoned her mother.

"Hi Mum, thanks for the invitation; are you sure you should be doing this in view of Dad's medical condition?"

"Oh don't be silly dear, your father is looking forward to it and it's really perked him up in actual fact."

"But wouldn't a gentle trip on the Orient Express have been more relaxing for you both to celebrate?"

"Not at all, your father has enjoyed toiling over his legendary home-made sausage rolls and has now put over one hundred of them in the freezer!" Priscilla chirped happily.

Chloe knew there was no reasoning with her mother once she'd decided to do something and as usual she felt she was just wasting her breath. She ended the call with an offer to bring a contribution for the party but was quickly reassured that everything was already organised.

Two weeks later, wearing her green velvet party frock, Chloe found herself driving through the Sussex countryside towards the village of Longoaks where she had grown-up.

139

A confetti of autumn leaves danced across her windscreen as she reminisced about all the wonderful country walks she and her father had enjoyed over the years with Teazel their Labrador. Her mother was never really into the great outdoors like they were but preferred a trip to the beauty parlour whilst Chloe and her father went on their hikes. Harold had always been a very fit and active man and together they had completed the whole length of the south downs way several times.

As she approached her parents' house Chloe noticed that the line of evergreens had become so tall they completely obscured the chimney pot. Pulling into the driveway, Evergreen House looked the same as when she last visited eleven months ago but now the garden was covered in a pretty netting of ochre and rust autumn leaves. The line of old conifer trees which had given the house its name still stood proudly around the garden perimeter, peering down over her like ancient guardians.

A cold shiver trembled across her shoulders as she remembered the last time she'd visited, just before she set off travelling to Australia. She had popped into her father's bedroom mid-morning to say her farewells and sat down beside his bed watching him sleep. His breathing was laboured and slow. As she caressed his gaunt wrinkled hand, a tear hovered upon her cheek before completing its journey by bouncing down and causing her father to stir. He slowly opened his eyes and smiled as he looked up into his daughter's face.

"I'm so sorry my dearest Chloe, I can't seem to get out of bed before noon these days," he said with a vague smile. "Then I fall asleep during the afternoon in my armchair, and go to bed immediately after supper. I don't know how your mother puts up with me. Now, talk to me about your forthcoming trip please sweetheart?"

Chloe slowly ran through her itinerary but after a while she realised her father had faded again and wasn't really concentrating, he seemed so consumed by weariness. Eventually his paper thin eyelids closed over his bulging eyes like a fragile injured bird. At that moment she mentally said farewell to him forever, firmly believing that she probably would never see him again. It was a bitter pill to swallow. As she drove back to the city, she couldn't stop the cascade of hot tears stinging tracks down her face.

Chloe had deliberately arrived at the party a few hours early to help with preparations and was aiming to take some of the stress off her seventy year old parents' shoulders. Apprehensively she dragged her suitcase from the boot and rang the doorbell.

"Darling!" gushed her mother. "You're early, how nice."

Priscilla was doused in her usual Chanel No. 5 perfume and her silver hair had been elaborately piled up on top of her head with a sparkly diamanté clip.

"You look lovely, Mum. How's Dad doing?" Chloe asked as she gave her mother a peck on the cheek.

"Harold dear," her mother called out, "Chloe's arrived."

Her father suddenly appeared at the doorway looking very dapper in a pale blue suit and blue velvet bow tie. His outfit was nothing like anything Chloe had ever seen him wear before, it was definitely not his usual style. As she went to hug him he quickly turned tail and dashed nimbly back towards the kitchen claiming that his devils on horseback were burning.

"You look very well, Dad," Chloe said as she caught up with him. "You've gained a bit of weight haven't you?"

"Yes, dear," interrupted her mother. "He's been on this fabulous new regime given by the doctor, haven't you Harold? He's really got his old spark back and has so much energy these days!"

Chloe was both amazed and relieved by the apparent improvement in her father's health. As she followed her mother into the dining room she was quite flabbergasted by the huge amount of food displayed on their long table. There were balloons (all evidently inflated by her father's breath), banners and streamers everywhere.

"Your father has done all this completely single-handedly," Priscilla proudly told Chloe before she disposed of her apron and mounted the stairs to get her party dress on.

Chloe went back into the kitchen to strike up a conversation with her father.

"I'm so pleased to see you looking so well, Dad. What's been your secret?" Chloe asked.

"Sorry dear, but every second counts before our guests start arriving; let's try and catch-up tomorrow shall we? I'll carry your bag up to your room for you."

Feeling confused and rejected, Chloe shadowed her father as he ran energetically up the stairs carrying her case. Although she was relieved to see her father looking so well, she felt there was something not quite right about him, but she couldn't quite put her finger on exactly what was.

"Gosh Dad, have you had painters and decorators in recently?" Chloe asked, looking around the guest bedroom.

"Oh no, it didn't take me long. The whole place needs renovating really but at least I've completed upstairs for now."

Chloe was dumbfounded. Eleven months ago her beloved father was close to death and now he seemed to have more strength and energy than he had ever had in the past. However, something about his behaviour disturbed her and she felt he had become cold and insensitive towards her, which made her feel sad.

After carefully unpacking the gifts she had bought for her parents and the new novel she'd been reading on the aeroplane, Chloe went down to find out where the music was coming from. There in the sitting room her parents were singing to each other as her father swept his wife across the floor in a Tango step. She stood at the door watching in amazement.

"I didn't know you could dance Dad, I've never seen that before," she said as the couple ended their sequence with her mother leaning backwards, a red rose held between her teeth.

"What do you think darling?" her mother asked. "We've been to classes together and are planning to entertain our guests when the champagne is served.

"I think it's wonderful," Chloe said, unconvinced. "I'll serve the champagne for you."

The evening was very lively with her parents dancing and her father uncharacteristically socialising and being the perfect host. There were many new friends at the party that Chloe hadn't met before and most of them appeared to be much younger than her parents. Chloe went to chat with her father's best friend Brian who was standing in the corner watching the proceedings with a peculiar look on his face. She knew his wife had died recently of heart problems and offered him her condolences.

"Thanks Chloe. Brenda wasn't as lucky as Harold; she too was waiting for a heart transplant but died before one became available for her."

"I didn't know…" Chloe said bewildered. "I had no idea."

Her father's dramatic health improvement now became clear to Chloe, but neither of her parents had told her about the transplant operation. She felt very hurt and decided to go to bed with the novel she had just bought; everything had become a little too much for her to take in.

After a sleep full of vivid dreams about her childhood, Chloe rose in the morning to a peaceful house and, believing her parents were still sleeping, took a shower in the immaculate new bathroom. Creeping downstairs with the intention of clearing up after the party, she found the house in a completely tidy condition. Her father was at the sink still washing up.

"Dad, have you done all this?" Chloe asked.

"It didn't take long dear. Coffee?" he replied, without look at her.

At last Chloe hoped she could sit and chat with her father in the quietness of the kitchen but soon her mother appeared in her dressing gown. As her father placed two cups of coffee in front of the women, he made his apologies and told them he needed to have a quick shower himself. When Harold had left the room her mother grabbed on to her daughter's hand with a grave look on her face.

"Look darling, I didn't tell you about your father's operation as I didn't want to worry you whilst you were so far away. You see, he nearly died and was so close to death, I didn't know what to do for the best."

"Oh, I'm sorry Mum, you've been through so much," Chloe said squeezing her hand reassuringly. "I would have got the next plane home to come and support you."

"I know dear," her mother smiled sweetly. "But there was a decision to be made that only I could make. You see, there wasn't a suitable donor available when your father entered his coma."

"Coma?" asked Chloe.

"Yes, and the doctors were worried that every second counted before he would lose more and more brain cells. They had to act quickly…"

There was a protracted pause as her mother's eyes filled with tears.

"I took the option for him to receive a robotic heart… and several robotic implants into his brain to prevent any further memory loss."

Chloe was speechless as her mind absorbed everything her mother was telling her. So much of it explained her father's new characteristics and behavioural changes. Her mother continued to tell her that the robotic implants would automatically update as Harold aged and keep him physically and mentally in peak condition, albeit that he would gradually, year by year, lose the personality he once had. Chloe's sobs began to fill the stillness of the room and her mother began crying along with her as they hugged each other.

"Now then, dear, I think we should both go for a walk and get some fresh air, don't you?" her mother said handing over a box of tissues. "I'll just get dressed and bring our coats."

"And just think dear," her mother added as she was leaving the room. "He will be Mr. Evergreen forever now; and the consolation is that you won't need to care for me in my dotage, your father can do that. In fact, he will probably be able to look after you in your old age too!"

About the author
Jeanne Davies' short stories have been published in anthologies by Bridge House, the Waterloo Festival, *Graffiti* Magazine, Centum Press, Earlyworks Press, Wadars and has been shortlisted by Vernal Equinox & Ink Tears. In 2020 Bridge House published *Drawn by the Sea,* her first single author collection. The stories in this collection were conceived while she walked with her dogs for miles in the magnificent green spaces of the Sussex countryside or wandering along the seashore with the serenity and chaos of the ocean, which provides great inspiration and peace.

Top of the Tree

Russell Heidorn

They waited, buried in a box deep in the storage room beneath summer clothes and old toys. Through a hole in the side, they watched as the snow fell leisurely out the window, covering the ground like heaven. The time was nearing once again and soon the box would be dragged out and the children would plunge in, choosing who gets to put up what. The trimmings could hardly wait.

At the bottom of the box were two stars.

Ever since the family's eldest son was born, the first star had been on top of the tree. He perched there every year watching the family sprout and grow. He remembered the first years, when the apartment was bare and the presents were rare, but love and laughter filled the space all the same.

Every year as they placed the star on top, he could see the changes the previous year had brought. He witnessed three more children enter into the family as the small apartment grew to a bungalow, then a rambler, and finally a two-story big enough to host the Christmas gathering. The house would be filled with family and friends and enough presents to bury half the tree. The kids would play games by the fire while the aroma of Grandma's fresh-baked ginger cookies would fill the air.

It was bittersweet when the oldest son moved out on his own. He returned every Christmas, but it wasn't the name. The family was growing, changing. The star saw the good times when the house bustled with the euphoria of the season, and the sad times like the year Grandma passed away and each family member made a special ornament to remember her.

New Year's Day was when the family packed up the decorations. Part of the tradition was to declare their resolutions as the New Year promised new beginnings. The star grieved as he went back into hibernation. But soon Thanksgiving would come and the box would be brought out again and he would see who had kept their promises and who didn't.

But last year was different. The star had not been pulled out of the box. Instead, he remained at the bottom with the other aging and unused lights and ornaments.

The second star was brand new last year and served his first time on top of the tree. For him everything was new and exciting. He swayed as the family sang Christmas songs while trimming the tree. He wept with joy as everyone came including the oldest son with his new wife. He laughed when the father dressed up as Santa but failed to fool the kids. He watched with wonder as the family opened gifts, shared their dreams and filled the home with love and laughter. It was all so fantastic and by New Year's Day when he was placed alongside the old star, he was exhausted.

As the box sat untouched through the dreary long summer, the two stars had a long talk. The elder knew his reign was done. He was too old and fragile now to be used. He would remain in the box listening to stories each year from the new star until the time would come when he would go to that sacred place where all decorations go. That was the way of things.

The old star taught the young star well. He taught patience, compassion and joy. He taught how to capture to the family's prayers and channel them up to Heaven. The young star listened, slowly learning what it really meant to be a Christmas star. And as the season approached, the old star knew the young star was truly ready to take his place on the top of the tree.

"One final question?" the young star asked one day.

"Of course," the old star answered.

"Last year, late one night, the youngest daughter came up to me. She said she prayed more than anything to see her grandmother again. She asked me why she prays and prays but God never answers her."

"He always answers," the old star replied. "But sometimes the answer is no."

Just then the light in the storage room came on. The mother and father walked in, dug through the clutter and dragged out the Christmas box. They very carefully sifted through the decorations until they pulled out the old star.

"It just needs a little TLC," the mother said.

"Let me see," the father replied. "Sure, I'll just strengthen the joints with a little hot glue and it'll be good as new."

"You know, we got this the year he was born," the mother said. "And now that his first baby is on the way, it will be their first Christmas star."

"It's the perfect gift," the father said.

"Oh, and I was thinking I might try making my mom's ginger cookies this year."

"That would be great. It'll be just like she's here with us again."

As they carried the star out of the room, the old star looked at the new star with a reborn smile.

"And sometimes, the answer is yes," was all the young star said.

About the author

Russell Heidorn lives in suburban Minneapolis and scatters his time between working and family while pursuing his dream of writing. He is currently working on a novel about a suburban man who scatters his time between work and family while pursuing his dream of writing.

Two Tiny Green Frogs

Margaret Bulleyment

I think of myself as the Ultimate Artist. I don't go into details of what I do, so if anyone asks, I'm just an artist and designer and then I move on quickly, before they ask me to paint their pet cat.

It's not I'm embarrassed by what I do – quite the opposite – but it just gets too complicated as in, "If you need me, you'll never meet me and I'll only know you, from what your family and friends tell me."

Sometimes, I wonder if the person a family describes, is really that person, or just what the family wants them to be. Either way, I create what they want.

Mine is a quality product – none of that football-coloured wrapround nonsense. You get a hand-painted, perfectly balanced design, on the coffin, or casket, of your choice. I prefer coffins, as they have six sides and are aesthetically, more pleasing. I take pride, in creating a complete work of art for the deceased person – whoever they may be – even, if they never see it.

Nowadays, I do get a few people planning in advance. They say it makes everything easier, for both them and their families. It takes more time, but I don't mind that, as it lifts my work to a whole new level. I keep more detailed notes and recordings, of my pre-arrangers. People are not computer data and I need to feel attached to living people, to understand my dead ones.

Anna, was one of those people. She came to see me in June, last year – late seventies, smartly dressed, lovely hands and jewellery. She said nothing about her health, like pre-arrangers usually do, but just that she wanted to get it right for the family. I told her that she was the most

149

important person, the family came second and then, I just let her talk.

She'd been a modern languages teacher, she loved music, sang in choirs and she and her husband, Jan, had enjoyed travelling – lakes and mountains, as they were not sun worshippers – to Switzerland, Austria, Norway and other scenic places.

Fjords, mountains and music, were floating around my head as I listened and loving those countries too, I warmed to her.

She loved her daughter, Sophie and her grandson, Danny. She admitted, Sophie had had problems in her life, but Anna and Jan had helped her through them and they loved Danny, dearly.

After Jan died, Anna had begun to investigate her family history and like everyone, once she'd begun, she wondered why she'd not started earlier. My professional response of course, was that she'd been too young and active, to care about the past.

Her parents had been Finnish, but she'd never known her father, as he'd died in Lapland in 1945. Anna was born in Helsinki, six months later, but her mother left Finland soon afterwards to live with a relative in London, so baby Aina, grew up as English, Anna.

She'd laughed when she'd told me that. "If I had known I'd meet a man called Bell, I might have stuck with Aina and saved hours of my life, not saying, 'Anna Bell is my whole name.' "

"In a few weeks' time," she continued, "when it's school summer holidays, I'm taking Sophie and Danny to the Arctic Circle, so we can find out more about my dear father, right where he lived and died, in Rovaniemi."

"How old's your grandson, Anna?" I'd asked her.

"He's twelve, so it won't matter that in July, we won't

see Joulupukki and his elves. When we get back, I'll sort out everything I've discovered about who my father was, and who I am. We'll go from there."

In September I received an email:

From: sophiefoster@gmail.com
Subject: Anna Bell
10 Sept 10.20
To: fayifeld@btinternet.com

Good morning, Ms Ifield

I'm sorry to have to tell you that sadly, my mother, Anna Bell, died from pancreatic cancer, last week. It was mercifully quick.

I'd no idea she'd begun to organise her funeral, while she was still alive. She left me a folder with copies of everything she'd discussed with you and some final wishes, she'd never got around to sharing with you, for her coffin design.

I also have a lot of paperwork to read and instructions from her, not to arrange her funeral until I've gone through it all with you.

Can I make an appointment to see you in a couple of weeks' time, please? She wanted a birch coffin. I'm not sure if they're difficult to come by, so might that add a further delay?

I'll have to bring my son with me. I hope that's all right.

Thank you for your help.

Regards

Sophie Foster

Sophie looked very flustered when she turned up, clutching a battered cardboard box – hair all over the place, no makeup, scruffy trainers and wearing a baggy sweater, several sizes too large. Danny lolloped in behind her, smiling all over his face, a sketchbook tucked under his arm.

Sophie pushed him down into a chair and dropped the box on the floor. "I'm sorry this is so complicated, Ms Ifield. Did Mum tell you she was ill, when she came to see you? Did she know then? I mean what…"

"Please call me Fay, Sophie. First of all, my sincerest condolences on your loss. I only knew your mother, briefly, but that glimpse into her life makes me eager to learn more, so we can give her the send-off, she deserves.

"She said nothing about being ill – just that you were all heading to Lapland, to find out more about her father. Perhaps, we could start with you telling me about that trip and what you discovered."

"It was awesome," burst out Danny. "It was the longest train journey ever, from Hells-inky, to Roving… Lapland… but there were these cool lounges with revolving seats and I've never seen so many trees and lakes and rocks… trees and lakes and rocks… and… birch trees and Christmas trees and… it was light all the time. We had blackout curtains in our bedrooms."

"That's enough, Danny," said Sophie, laying a restraining hand on his arm.

"Sophie, if you don't mind, I'd really like to hear Danny's version of his trip with his grandmother. I know he was a very important part of her life."

"I've brought my sketchbook to show you," said Danny, sliding it across the table and proudly opening it. "Look, that's the Arctic Circle sign, outside the Santa Claus

Village. Gran took a selfie of us all there, but I like to sketch things.

"She was very grumpy, when we got inside the Village. She said it was touristy and it was disrespectful, building it on the site of a German barracks. It should have a Finnish name too, not an American-Dutch one. The Finnish sounds like, *You're-all-pukey,* or something."

He paused for breath.

"Danny," said Sophie, "for goodness' sake…"

"When we got back from *You're-all-pukey's* Village," Danny continued. "We went straight to the hotel in Rovy and then Gran bought some flowers and we walked up to the churchyard. There were masses and masses of little gravestones, like paving stones, in the grass. Some had funny writing on them, which Gran said was Russian. Each stone had a rosebush planted beside it and we wandered around until Gran found the grave she was looking for and put the flowers on it. The writing on the stone was in Finnish, but I could see the name was Mikko Aalt-onen. My middle name's Michael, but my Mikey, is spelt differently. I'd rather be called Mikey, than Danny.

"Then we all sat down on a bench and Gran told me that my great-grandfather, Mikko, had been born in a place called Vipery, but it was now called something else and in a different country. He'd fought to get his country back and died doing it. I thought she'd be sad, but she said she was happy at having found him. A lot of men were unidentified. Then we walked back to the grave and Gran picked the flowers up and said that you weren't meant to leave flowers there, but she'd had to do it. A lot of the stones didn't have any bodies under them."

"This next bit's complicated, Fay," said Sophie. "I'm not sure even now, I've got it right.

"Mikko was born in Viipuri, in Karelia, which in those

153

days was Finland, on the Russian border. His family moved to the north, ending up near Rovaniemi, in Finnish Lapland. The Russian invasion in the winter of 1939, when Mikko was twenty-five, ended with the Finns signing a peace treaty, with the Russians... Soviet Union... or whatever you want to call them... which left Finland a sovereign country, but in return, Karelia and the borderlands became part of the Soviet Union.

"Then in 1944, there was a second war, when the Finns allied with the Germans, in the hope of getting Karelia back. So, thousands and thousands of Germans poured into Lapland, to confront the Russians, but the Russians demanded Finland expel them. The Russians advanced and the Germans retreated, to Norway, destroying everything on the way. Rovaniemi and all its beautiful old buildings was burned to the ground and Mikko died there."

"So, who were the goodies and who were the baddies?" asked Danny.

"Who knows," said Sophie. "Outside, Rovaniemi, there's another cemetery – a German one – with another two and a half thousand bodies of young men, not much older than you, who also died for their country."

There was an awkward pause.

Danny turned another page of his sketchbook. "This page is all reindeers and over here, is a sketch map of Rovy, which was rebuilt in the shape of reindeers' antlers. Isn't that fantastic?"

"It's reindeer, Danny, not reindeers," said Sophie.

"But there's a lot of them," said Danny. "I loved the reindeer farm. We went down the river, in a big wooden boat with a flat bottom and our own boatman. It was a lovely sunny afternoon, but they'd made us wear waterproof jackets with hoods, dungaree thingys and wellies. It took us half an hour, but after five minutes, the weather changed and it bucketed down. Even with all our special gear on, the water poured down our necks and backs and we ended up with squelchy pants. It was horrible. We climbed out on to the river bank, sank into the mud and walked up the duckboards to the farm, looking like drowned rats. "I know, we could have gone in a 4x4," said Gran, when a Japanese family stepped out of one, as dry as Weetabix, "but this was part of our Lapp adventure."

"The reindeers made up for it. They were lovely – so soft and cuddly – but the Japanese boy, looked terrified. I took his hand and showed him how to stroke them, very gently. His parents nodded and smiled at us. Then we went into the Lapp tent and were given reindeer's milk. It was very creamy and the Lapp man made a reindeer mark, on my forehead, with a stick from the fire and said, I was now a Sami Lapp. This sketch is the tent and the Lapp man, in his Lapp clothes. I liked his Four Winds hat, red, for the sun and blue, for the moon. The word for reindeer is *boazu*. Rudolph the Red-Nosed Boazu? Isn't that funny?

"Then we went into the Lapp man's proper house and had coffee, cake and cloudberries. I love cloudberries. I ate them every day in Lapland – they were everywhere. They look like shiny, golden blackberries, but taste much nicer. We had a whole dish called cloudberry perfect, after we had been to the graveyard – with lots of cream. I drew it – here." He poked his finger at the sketch.

"This last page is the Forestry Museum. That's a little timber cabin, the lumberjack people lived in. Gran said Mikko had worked in a logging company, before the war, but he was something to do with the new machines that cut down the trees. Tree in Finnish, is *puu*. Gran was teaching me more funny Finnish words."

"Danny, please stop, before you drive us completely mad," pleaded Sophie.

"You know something, Danny," I said. "I think with your mum's permission, you and I will both design your gran's coffin. What do you think?"

"I'd love that. I can, can't I, Mum?"

Sophie gave me a strange look, but agreed. "Danny, I don't think we need all of this box, so take my keys and put the rest of these folders in the car, please. Why don't you leave that sketchbook with Fay, so she can look through it, before our next appointment."

Sophie dropped her voice, as Danny left. "Thank you so much, Fay, but you don't have to do this. I'm confused. Danny is sad and missing his gran, but the trip seems to have given him a new confidence and he never stops talking about trees and reindeer... well, you can see that, for yourself."

"Yes. This is all part of Anna's life and legacy, which I want to capture. His sketchbook, ideas and enthusiasm, will be very useful."

"That's good. Next, I need to get quite a bit of paperwork translated – Anna was the linguist, not me – and when I've done that, I'll make another appointment."

From: sophiefoster@gmail.com
Subject: Anna Bell
27 Sept 19.30
To: fayifeld@btinternet.com

Good evening, Fay

I've got some of Anna's paperwork translated and I don't think that Mikko was the person we all thought he was.

Can I see you without, Danny? Perhaps in my lunch hour this week? I work near your office.

156

Somewhere between 1.00 and 2.00 any good?

Sorry to make your life difficult.

Sophie

From: fayifeld@btinternet.com
Subject: Lunch tomorrow?
27 Sept 20.10
To: sophiefoster@gmail.com

Sophie,

I can do tomorrow, if that's easier. The River Café, down by the bridge at 1.00?

The birch coffin is arriving at the end of the week, so you can start planning the funeral properly with my funeral director, Tim, and then at the beginning of next week, Danny and I can finish designing and start painting it.

Fay

Sophie was already seated at a table, overlooking the river, by the time I got there. She looked slightly less dishevelled, than the last time I had seen her, but was noticeably agitated.

"Can this get any more difficult, Fay?"

"Everyone has a different story – that's how I make a living."

"Here we go then," she began. "Mikko was on the management board of a timber business, located near the Forestry Museum, we visited. He was part – what we'd now call – a technical translator. Mum said he had a gift for languages. She told us the logging machines came in from America, so he must have spoken good English; he was born near Russia; he

157

spoke his native language and Swedish, Finland's second language and also some German.

"In her personal files, with her birth and marriage certificates, Mum also had her father's certificates and the letter her mother had received after he'd died, which thanks him posthumously, for his service to his country. That letter came from the Finnish Intelligence Service."

"So...?"

"There's more, Fay," said Sophie rummaging in her bag. "What do you think this is?"

"An ancient little clutch bag, made of very soft leather."

"Yes. So why would it have two more letters in it – not in Mum's file – one from the German Intelligence Service and another, from the Russian Intelligence Service? Both letters were sent to Helsinki, but arrived in London, after the war."

"Go ahead and say it, Sophie."

"This bag was my grandmother's and Mikko, has to have been a spy. What other explanation is there?"

"But how on earth, could he have juggled all those different intelligence services?"

"Circumstances changed quickly, didn't they, Fay. And everything's grey, not black and white. One minute, the Germans and Finns are friends and then they're not. What bothers me, is that Mum thought Mikko was this great Finnish hero and perhaps, he wasn't. We're presenting her life as a hero's daughter and she wasn't. Worst of all, what do we tell Danny?"

"I think, Danny would be thrilled to know his ancestor was a spy. You could tell him that, without the questionable details, surely?

"Look, Sophie, you're not the first person to discover their relative was not who they thought they were. I've come across secret families; children, told their parents had died so someone else would look after them; bigamy, incest and all sorts of horrendous crimes, which register higher up the Deceived Scale, than participation in a war, in a country with very loose borders."

"But Danny's so excited about his Finnish heritage," replied Sophie, "and he identifies with his grandmother, as she grew up without a dad too."

"Your son is far more resilient than you think. His Finnish heritage is in his blood, whatever's happened. And anyway, we don't know what the intelligence was, do we? Mikko could have been far more patriotic, than we think. We're never going to know, so let's give him the benefit of the doubt and just add that to the 'rich tapestry' of your mother's life."

"Perhaps, you're right," said Sophie, reluctantly.

"How's the funeral service coming along? When Tim told me the coffin had arrived, he said you'd booked the date. In a fortnight?"

"Yes, and you won't be surprised to hear, that it'll be wall to wall Sibelius – in, to the choral version of *Finlandia*, sung by Mum's choir friends and out, through the curtains, to the *Karelia Suite*. Danny loves to 'conduct' *Karelia,* so it might be quite a spectacle. You're very welcome to attend, or is that not a professional thing to do?"

"Not usually."

"Well, if you're not doing anything this Sunday afternoon, you're welcome to join Danny and I, here, for some cake and before that, if it's fine, we'll walk along the river and through the wood and back. We both have birthdays next week and we usually have a little celebration together, the weekend before, when school and work don't get in the way."

"What a good idea."

Sunday dawned brightly, so I threw my walking shoes into the car and drove down to the River Café.

Before I'd stepped out of the car, Danny was hurtling towards me across the car park. "We're going back! We're going back!"

"Let's walk," said Sophie leading the way. "You'll never guess what Mum has done."

"Gran has given us tickets to go back to Lapland, at Christmas," bellowed Danny. "We'll see reindeers in the snow!"

"Can you believe, she even made sure I could get off work, then?" exclaimed Sophie, "although my office manager, is an old pupil of hers."

"We're going to see the Northern Lights!!!"

"It's not guaranteed, Danny, don't get too excited."

"We opened our presents this morning," announced Danny. "Mum had some jewellery and books. I had four books – trees; reindeer; Lapland and miffology. Then I opened a reindeer head – not a real one, a soft one – that you hang on the wall and a tiny frog (that was a special joke between Gran and me.) Then, we got right to the bottom of the box and there was a big envelope, with our names on and inside, were all the tickets."

"That's wonderful, Danny," I replied. "Your gran was a very thoughtful person."

Sophie and I tramped on through the wood, with Danny cavorting around us.

"I'm sitting down here," he announced, "and talking to the trees. Look at these roots, they're like arms wrapped around me. It says in my new book that trees talk to each other, through their roots – The Wood Wide Web. Do you believe that?"

"They certainly communicate," I agreed. "It's something to do with... fungus? I also read that larger trees protect smaller ones that don't get sufficient light, by sending sugars and nutrients to them, along the underground root systems.

"People connect through their roots, so why not trees," I added.

"What do you mean?"

"Well, your gran has connected her father to her, even though she didn't know him and then, to your mum and then, down to you."

"My dad doesn't connect down to me," snorted Danny. "He sends me money for my birthday and Christmas, but we never see him. He loves his computers more than us."

"He's still your father, Danny and he's given you his name. Do you know what it means?

"What Foster... means?"

"It's a short version of Forester. A long way back, before computers, your dad's side of the family was connected to trees.

So, I've got double tree roots?"

"Something like that."

"Cool, but can we go back and eat cake now?"

"That's an excellent idea.

"Now, I'm finishing the coffin background, tomorrow and then on Tuesday, you can help me put in the details. Sophie, you may want to stay up in the office with a coffee, while Danny and I crawl around the studio getting covered in paint."

I was pleased with my background – I'd finally managed to blend a variety of trees, mountains, fjords, lakes and something vaguely resembling Sibelius's house, into a four seasons panorama.

Danny looked at it critically. "Could that tree have big roots, like the one in the wood? The one with arms?"

"That shouldn't be a problem, Danny. I can do that, while you finish off the reindeer and then you can start on the cloudberries.

"There's something I wanted to ask you. What languages did your gran teach?"

"German at the high school," Danny replied. "Russian at the college and she was learning Finnish and teaching me some words."

"That's what I thought and when you were in Rovaniemi, did she spend a lot of time in the archives, or museums, or did she spend most of her time with you and your mum?"

"With us."

"I don't think your gran went to find out about her father, Danny. I think she'd already done that online and just went so that you were all together, seeing the places he'd lived in and died in."

"Mum said he was some kind of spy. Isn't that fantastic!"

He dropped his paintbrush and ran across to his bag, in the far corner. "There's something very important, we have to do," he said plunging his arm in and pulling out a small package, which he carefully unwrapped, to reveal two tiny, green frog toys.

"I saw Gran buy these when we were at the Christmas Village. A week before she died, she gave me this package to open. She said I wasn't to tell Mum, but she wanted me to put one of the frogs, in her coffin. She said Mum would think it a revolting idea, but Gran thought that I understood my Finnish heritage, better than Mum did.

"Where great-grandfather came from, it was an old tradition to make a tiny coffin, put a dead frog in it and put the frog coffin, inside the coffin of the person who'd died. The frog soaked up all the bad things that person and their 'cestors had done in their lives, so it was a fresh start for the new gen'rations.

"She said I needed to make a coffin, the size of my hand

162

and I would have to ask you, to help me put the froggy coffin into her coffin. She told me Mum didn't know she'd started to plan her funeral, with you and I wasn't to tell that either. The other frog, she would put into my birthday parcel and when I opened it, it would remind me of what I'd done.

"So, I made this coffin, out of cardboard." He reached into his bag again and pulled out his handiwork. "I thought I could put some birch shavings, from the floor, inside it."

"Nothing's going inside, anywhere," shouted Sophie, bursting into the room, snatching the tiny coffin from Danny's hands and hurling it into the corner.

"A revolting idea? Yes, it is, but what's most revolting is that you," she spat at me, "hide secrets in my mother's coffin. She's my mother, not yours and Danny's my son, not yours.

"You're like those mythological hags, who spin, measure and snip off peoples' lives, except you, claw up the threads and wind them into your own sad little life. Your life is so miserable, you have to live other peoples."

"Mum, Mum, it's not like that," screamed Danny, as Sophie ran from the room. "You've got to listen."

He blundered after her.

"I was listening and I heard too much," Sophie shouted back, stepping out on to the street.

Tim flung open the connecting door. "What on earth's happening, Fay? I'm trying to talk to grieving people in here."

"I'm so sorry, Tim. I'll sort it out as quickly as possible."

Outside, there was no sign of either Danny, or Sophie, but there was some sort of commotion on the road, down by the traffic lights.

I hurried over and pushed through the gathering crowd. Danny was lying motionless in front of a car, Sophie bending over him. Some people were even taking pictures, for Christ's sake! I should have rushed to help, but I froze.

"He charged straight across the road, just as the lights changed," said the woman, next to me. "He was shouting after that woman beside him. I feel sorry for the driver."

I ran back into the funeral director's and upstairs to my office. From the window, I saw the ambulance arrive and then scream off into the distance. I felt sick. I wandered downstairs into the studio, picked up Danny's frogs and the tiny coffin, locked the studio door and left.

From: fayifeld@btinternet.com
Subject: Danny
5 Oct 23.55
To: sophiefoster@gmail.com

Sophie,

Please, please tell me that Danny is all right. I've tried to phone you and I understand why you aren't answering, but please tell me what's happening.

I cannot apologise enough for everything's that happened. Yes, I have taken a lot of interest in your mother, you and Danny.

The truth is, I had a brother, just like Danny – special needs and all those stupid labels – who died of sepsis, when he was ten. Danny reminds me so much of him, that I got too involved in your family's story.

You are right. It's your story – not mine.

Please tell me that Danny is not seriously injured and then you'll not hear from me again.

I am so, so sorry.

Fay

From: sophiefoster@gmail.com
Subject: Danny
6 Oct 00.30
To: fayifeld@btinternet.com

Fay

Danny's recovering well. Fortunately, the car was going slowly enough, not to have done him any lasting harm.

I'm the one who should be apologising. I'm so sorry about the death of your brother.

Please forgive me for my cruel words. I know nothing about your life and I shouldn't have spoken to you like that. I'm the one with the sad life. Who has a job because of someone their mother taught? I would like all three of us to meet up again, so we can rewind our story. I hope you'll agree to this.

I've altered the funeral date, so that when Danny's recovered, he'll be able to help you with finishing the coffin and then Danny and I can put the frog coffin inside it – together.

I'll let you know when he's fit enough to do that.

Please forgive me, Fay

Sophie

To: fayifeld@btinternet.com
Subject: Painting!
13 Oct 19.00
From: sophiefoster@gmail.com

Hi Fay

I feel fantastic!!!!!!!!!!!!!!

I'm SOOOOOOOOOOOOOOOOOOOO happy we're coming back on Tuesday to finish Gran's coffin.

Frog coffin?????????????? Can I make another one?????????????????

See yer,

D

Sophie and Danny greeted me with warm hugs.

"The good news," I announced, "is that I found the frog and Tim has cut to size some leftover little pieces of birch, so all you have to do, Danny, is glue them together, to make a matching mini coffin."

"Yeah! I'll do that now."

"Danny told me that you thought Mum had already researched her father," said Sophie. "I think I agree with you now – the frog coffin explains everything."

With the tiny coffin drying, Danny painstakingly, added the final touch to the cloudberries. "These are good enough to eat."

"He said… modestly," laughed Sophie.

"He's quite a talented young artist. Look at the translucence of those berries. You should be so proud of him, Sophie.

"Now, here's the birch shavings and the frog… and then

both of you need to put the frog coffin, inside our great work of art," I said, flicking on my CD player.

Sophie and Danny carefully placed the tiny object in its final resting place, as *Karelia* resounded around the room.

"Great!" shouted Danny, conducting wildly. "Pom, POM-paa-paa-pom, Pom POM-paa-paa-pom..."

"Good job, Tim's out this afternoon," I shouted. "Now there's one final thing to do, Danny, and that's for you to paint a tiny frog, on the outside of your gran's coffin."

"Are you sure, you won't come to the funeral, Fay?"

"Thank you, Sophie, but no. It's Anna's ancestors' lives; her life; your life and Danny's life – not mine. I'll settle for a postcard of the Northern Lights. Enjoy your Joulu journey."

Danny was crouching on the floor. "Shall I paint the frog, down here, at the edge of the lake, by the Roots Tree?"

"Perfect, Danny. It's the final detail of your gran's life. You are the Ultimate Artist."

About the author
Margaret Bulleyment, a retired teacher from Oxfordshire, has had short stories published on story websites and in anthologies, including Bridge House's *CaféLit, Snowflakes, Baubles, Glit-er-ary, Crackers, Nativity* and *Mulling It Over*.

She has twice had short plays performed professionally, as a finalist in the Ovation Theatre Awards and her children's play *Caribbean Calypso* was runner-up in Trinity College of Music and Drama's 2011 International Playwriting Competition. It has been performed three times in Bangalore, by educational charity Jagriti Kids.

This year she was awarded second prize in the Fowey Festival Daphne du Maurier Short Story Competition, judged by Raynor Winn.

She enjoys choral singing and gardening, but fortunately for her neighbours, not at the same time.

Until We Are Ever Green

Georgina Wright

*"**Until** you see beauty everywhere, in every face, until then, you are blind."* **Kamand Kojouri**

With four rapid deep cuts the young Abeto was removed from the earth. Next with a shovel and a layer of damp soil Abeto was rammed into the smallest space imaginable and left alone. Really alone. The only life known was a nursery of togetherness. Abeto severed from sibling seedlings was shuddering with shock. Once finger like root points reached out for the tips of the others but now, were chopped off. After the sharp cuts came a terrible numb silence.

Until... Abeto, branches, trunk and roots were raised high above the earth. So, this was what it was like to move like a bird. But the roots were still in the prison like pot and shaken, the trunk was swaying and Abeto's leaves, thin and needle like on the branches were struggling to hang on. All of Abeto's many parts were in all the wrong places. High up vertical, horizontal and then upside down. Suddenly when bashed down onto the back of a large beast Abeto was upright again. The beast moved off creating an endless rush of air around the branches but leaving the smell of Abeto's first home far behind. That home was a place of safety and increasing awareness of many other living things. Some were furry, some feathered and some nibbled and nipped. Many more moved around creating a buzz or a flutter in the stillness of young trees growing up together. But this beast and others nearby sounded like giant flies going too fast on a collision course. This was not safe and Abeto's branches cried out at every bump.

Until... There was a feeling of gentle movement, being

lifted up, placed carefully and close to other trees. Abeto's roots recovering from their wounds reached out to the other roots that Abeto's fine thin leaves could sense nearby. The roots were trying hard to find a way but there was something impenetrable and so hard between them. And there, Abeto stood for many nights and days, in a stand of trees which was different from being in the nursery together. Their branches could touch but their roots were apart. Abeto's trunk felt strong again, less alone.

Until... Gradually all the other small young trees around Abeto were lifted away.

"That one's rather small for three years growth. Shall we reduce the price? It's the old type of Christmas tree and doesn't look that pretty in a pot."

"Needles last and stay green though. And such a fresh smell of pine."

"It's a silver fir tree not a pine. Guess the smell is similar though. But there are so many better varieties now. No one wants this kind anymore."

The harsh sounds faded into the distance. But alerted Abeto to the fate of trees that belonged to the human world. Seed knowledge was fading as was the future of forest each young tree aspired to grow tall into. Only the roots knew the old fears of trunks falling to the earth through human hands. But Abeto's roots were still there. All Abeto's parts were together even if alone and far from other trees. This was a different kind of fear. There was no falling but more lifting up again, tilting back and forth, all the branches tightly wrapped up. Abeto was bumped through air and the motion was frightening to no longer be a part of the earth. And worse was to come.

Abeto was finally placed down in the warmest spot ever known. Warmer than the light of the summer sun even though it was the cold light of winter. How could it be so warm? Abeto's leaves did not know what to breathe. It was suffocating and the roots were crying out for water. The leaves were tense, ready to drop.

Until… There was more movement. Abeto was pulled out from the dryness and carefully put into a bigger space, full of soft sweet-smelling earth. Suddenly the roots were drenched with a gush of cold water. The leaves breathed again. And then the most amazing thing happened. All over the branches tiny spots of sunlight were appearing even though there was the dark of night outside.

A young human child came close to Abeto touching the leaves, sniffing up the scent while calling out to another human figure. The child was happy and talking away to this caring presence. Was this the mysterious mother tree of the forest? The one that gave help to all the young trying to grow. The mother and the young one carefully hung bright shining balls on Abeto's branches. The touch was gentle through finger like roots. All of Abeto's withering was brightening into new life. It was if the mother tree was there giving water to the roots and a love never felt before. The lights were like the rays of sunshine playing around the branches. Abeto was alone but not alone. All was well with Abeto's world.

Until… One day Abeto was moved back into the world of wind, rain and even the cold white stuff that weighed the branches down. The days were dark and lights no longer played around the leaves and branches. The bright shining balls and the warmth that the leaves had adjusted to so well were all gone. The child did not visit or talk to Abeto and the sense of mother being close was gone too. Abeto was truly alone again.

Just as Abeto's roots were about to freeze in the icy waterlogged pot a human came and pulled Abeto out of the wet prison and placed the roots deep into a hole where the soil was good. The roots felt the warmth of being deep underground and the fear of drowning or worse freezing went away. The water could run deep into the soil here. Abeto's roots could sense other roots close by and were no longer alone. The branches could sway easily in the wind and the trunk did not fear toppling over. Abeto was deeply rooted again. But Abeto longed for the child and the lights on the branches. Abeto wanted to be inside and centre of attention again.

Each year at the turning of the light into short dark days there would be the pretty lights on inside but Abeto was always left outside and no child came close by to smell the freshness of the leaves or dress the branches with lights. Many of these small chattering beings went past him without even looking and hurried into the inside where the lights flashed and sparkled.

Abeto's only friends were the birds that came nearby and as he grew a bit taller and wider some like the bold robin would perch on him. One bird with a gold crest that shimmered on the top of its tiny head reminded Abeto of the lights. The visits of this very small bird brought joy. And yes, on asking it was called a goldcrest who was happy to peck away at small insects that irritated Abeto. Abeto was cared for again.

"Reach higher to the sky so I can safely use your branches to keep cats from my nest and weasels from my eggs."

Abeto's trunk stretched out, the branches reached out and the roots spread out. Abeto could care for the bird too. And so, the goldcrest made a nest and there was the sound of youngsters again. Abeto was enjoying life as a tree outside and the memory of the inside was fading.

Until… One day there were no more lights inside and there was a sadness resonating from the walls. No children visited. All was too quiet. Deadly quiet.

Through that year so many plants grew closer and closer to Abeto. There were the nettles and these had quite a rough edge to the leaves that could sting but worse were the brambles with thorns that wrapped around the lower branches and fought with the roots for space. There was a new sense of suffocating. Life was pricklier, harder and the roots struggled to reach out into the soil. But more birds came and enjoyed the fruits of black berries. One bird called the jackdaw mocked Abeto for still being such a small tree. The jackdaw boasted of the tall trees which scraped the clouds where she and her kind roosted. Abeto longed to be taller to escape the brambles and to live with other trees. All the roots wanted was to touch other tree roots.

And then there was mayhem in the garden. All the brambles were being pulled out. Some blackbirds gave out strong warning screeches and the roots of the brambles screamed. The brambles were torn up and thrown out of the garden. But Abeto could still sense some deep down under the roots and had no doubt they would be back. For a while he could be free of the strangling roots. Perhaps grow taller. All was well.

Until… There was a chatter from the humankinds. Abeto's branches drooped low.

"It will grow too big. Take it out now. It's boring there's no blossom. It's just another evergreen and it will create too much shade."

Abeto felt a wrenching, a tumbling. The roots were pulled out of the earth. Abeto's branches were touching the ground. The roots torn out were turned to the sky.

Abeto breathed with difficulty through the thin leaves. The roots gasped for water.

Until… There was some noise from children.

"Hey Jo, look there's a Christmas tree near the rubbish bins."

172

"But it's summer now not Christmas."

"Someone's thrown it out. If it's rubbish, can we take it?"

"It looks alive. It's still got most of its needles. Let's plant it and use it next Christmas."

"If it survives."

"Let's have a bit of hope. Be fun to have a real Christmas tree instead of that tiny plastic one Mum gets out every year."

Abeto was dragged along a hard track with no sense of earthly softness. And was left propped precariously against a wall.

There were cross voices and disappointed children.

"It's too big for inside the house and it's too big for the garden."

"It's someone else's rubbish. Take it back."

"And leave it to die?" wailed a tiny voice.

Abeto's insides were groaning, without any connection to the earth all the parts that made Abeto were slowly and painfully losing their life force. With some light there was the chance to breathe and make food but for how long? Abeto waited and withered.

Until… there was a kinder human voice and the cross words and crying stopped.

"I know what we can do, Jo. Wipe your tears, Janni. Look everyone, you know there's some tree planting going on near the school. This fir tree could go there. If it survives over the next few months, it will be the tallest and will give shelter to birds while the others grow stronger. It could be like the mother tree."

It was only a few days until the Christmas holidays, when some children wandered down the path from the school. The fir tree had survived the summer and grown new branches. There were other trees growing well close by. It was as if the taller tree helped by giving shelter from

173

the wind, and shade from strong sun. The children looked up and saw there were candle like cones. And was that a tiny bird with a flash of gold? Carefully on the lower branches the children hung some solar powered lights. All breathed in deep the most beautiful scent of a living silver fir tree. All was well with their worlds.

Until... many, many years later there was another angry dispute about this tall silver fir tree at a meeting in the school.

"It is too tall."

"Dangerous. Sways a lot in strong winds."

"It stops all the other trees growing."

"It's not indigenous. Native trees support wildlife."

Jo wanted to speak up and tell them they were wrong and that he had known this tree for almost 70 years of its life. And almost all of his own. But no one noticed a frail old man with a silver-grey beard raise his hand to speak. He turned to go. Who would want to listen to his story anyway? The story of how he and his friends saved the tree from the rubbish and how he and his grandfather planted it by the school. And wasn't it that strange little girl Janni and her family who started the tradition of hanging lights on the tree? There were a few voices in favour of keeping the tree but most of the children who grew up with the tree and sung around it at Christmas no longer lived nearby. In fact, there were very few of the community he grew up with left in the area. All seemed to move away. Janni's family were one of the first to go but he was told the children of the school still continued the tradition. But he wouldn't really know because he and his wife avoided being near young children.

One grey day in the distance Jo heard the sound of a chain saw. His cup of tea spilled all over him. He wiped his eyes with a grubby tea towel. There was no one to talk to.

174

He missed his wife. The loneliness of loss crept back into him and would not shift.

Until… He decided to walk up towards the school some months later. There was supposed to be a bench made from the planks of the silver fir tree. He was reluctant to see the space where the tree used to stand but wanted to make sure there was a bench. And there it was with its silvery wood bright in the sunshine of a chilly April day. He carefully sat down and the bench was warm from the sun. He breathed deep remembering his childhood, remembering the tree, wondering why all those years ago it had been thrown on the rubbish heap.

His grandfather, the local gardener who knew so much about plants and trees found the best place for it to grow. So, the silver fir tree had made it, to about 76. Wasn't that about the same age as when his grandfather died? They thought the tree was about six years old when they planted it together. The tree was always Jo's connection to his grandad. Was that his voice?

"Silver fir trees grow slowly at first but then can get very tall in the right conditions. Lots of birds love them for the shelter they give in the winter and the insects in the summer. With a good root system, they can live for over 200 years."

Jo was sure those were his grandfather's words but it was an elderly woman with a rather remarkable carved walking stick talking to a child.

"But they cut it down," Jo blurted out angrily.

"Why did they cut it down, Aunty Janni? It was our school's really real Christmas tree. We saw them cutting it down and our whole class cried so much that day."

"I don't know, but I know why we planted it." She gave Jo a reproachful look. He had upset the child with his words. Then her expression changed to that wide smile. She knew who he was.

175

Janni's eyes were as bright as Jo remembered and full of tears. Her tears saved that tree then, he was sure of that now. But his tears could not save what he loved.

"It's Jo, isn't it? I can't believe it." She turned to the child, a bit unsteady on her feet and held the child's hand.

"We used to all play together, all the children in the street. I was the youngest, always trailing behind and crying. We moved away when I went to Secondary but we always came back for the Christmas gathering around the tree."

"It's Janni isn't it? I remember those days clearer now than ever but forget what happened a week ago." His voice wavered, embarrassed. All the older children never took any notice of Janni, she was a nuisance trailing behind and forever crying. But her skin was noticeable and still the same with those patches of white and dark brown on her face. But her features, her eyes, her smile radiated warmth and beauty.

"But you, you look like your grandad. He was such a kind man and knew so much about plants and trees. And generous. He gave me some books on trees too, which I still have."

"Is that why you know all the names of trees, and do wood carvings, Aunty Janni?"

"Well, I guess that was the start of my love for trees. It's so good to see you, Jo. And perhaps you can help me. When I found out they were to cut the tree down, I asked for the bench and offered to design a sculpture for the stump. That tree was very important to all of us, evergreen and ever Christmas."

Jo's mood was lifting as he thought about the special lives his grandfather and the tree lived. He looked round at the sizeable stump of the tree. So, all the talk about creating a carving on it and the bench was Janni's doing. How did she manage to save something of the tree?

"I'm involved in a nature conservation group but if famous local trees are cut down, we make sure there can be some way to honour all they have given us. You were good at telling stories Jo. You should tell the story of this tree."

"But it's a sad story. Who wants a sad story? The tree could have lived another hundred or so years."

"I think your grandad once said that the roots stay alive especially if there is a large stump and help new seedlings to grow. That's why I asked for the stump to be left. I thought to design a mother and child shape. Or father? Do you have children?"

"No, err, yes, err." He always thought they didn't until he found his wife crying five years later on that day. "We lost a child, miscarriage. Err, and you?"

"I'm so sorry for you both, no, no children. I never married. Or no one wanted to marry me. My skin or maybe my high standards."

Jo sat at one end of the bench, Janni at the other end. The child wandered down to the fence in front of the disused railway line.

"Do you remember the railway? I remember my granddad being really sad when it closed. In his childhood the family could take the train into town or in the other direction out to the countryside and the hills."

"Well, there's lots of trees there now and lots of jackdaws too making lots of noise with their social chit chat. Did you know those birds are becoming rarer now? They need tall trees for good roosting places. And there are so many tiny goldcrests and those blue ones that creep down the trunk, nuthatches. That old railway is a great place for wildlife now."

Jo rubbed his eyes. Were these tears for what was gone? Or for the little he had done with his life?

"I thought I was the one for tears but look, look through the tears. What can you see down in that damp dark wood?"

177

Jo looked again. The child was pointing and grinning. "Auntie Janni knows her trees. Can you see it?"

There was a shape deep within the woodland like a fir tree, about the same size as the silver fir they dragged home that day. About six years old, perhaps? Yes, it was, it must be. And a little further under the dark canopy of trees? Yes, there was another one. Growing slowly, waiting for enough light. Tomorrow, he would bring his binoculars. There may be more. He sat back happier, not so alone.

"Now I've found you again we could put your grandfather's name on the bench. I'm sorry I never knew his real name. And my mother only ever knew him as the gardener. I was just going to put the tree's name. There will be an event for the children to help them as many were really upset when the tree was cut down. We can also show them how one tree is now two, maybe more in a wild wood. Thanks to male and female all in one."

Jo smiled. For all her tears Janni had always been a determined and creative spirit. Maybe he could share the story of that silver fir tree and his green fingered grandfather. He did not need to hide away in his house so much. The silver fir tree had found its forest and could grow until at least the next century. And until his time came, he could get on with living, maybe even loving again, and definitely he could help create the forest communities that trees longed to belong to.

A tale told on behalf of Abies alba, a silver fir tree (we/us).

About the author
Georgina has been involved with creative writing throughout her teaching career alongside teaching Literature, Media and Drama and is concerned about the creative arts in Education. On leaving the classroom she went to live in a Spanish woodland where she could learn more about the amazing diversity in nature and

pursue various writing projects. This has included a blog www.navasolanature.wordpress.com where she records this nature journey, some playful attempts at poetry and more seriously, writing short stories, a memoir and a completed novel with a sequel with mentoring from www.debzhobbs-wyatt.co.uk. Georgina is passionate about protecting nature and engaging young and old with the wonders of a wild world we may lose forever.

Watching Cormorants

Liz Cox

Martin no longer came to sit with her, although she waved to his window as she passed. The curtains were different now, a bright yellow which Martin would never have chosen. She missed his company, his bright conversation, his observations on the sea, the dogs, and the invading tourists. She smiled as she thought of some of his choice words, remembering the way they often shared a bag of chips from the chippy, dipping greasy, salty hands into the paper bag at the same time and rummaging around for the last chip.

June sat here on their favourite bench in front of the Monkey Puzzle tree in the marina each evening, admiring the greedy cormorants flashing their iridescent feathers as they skimmed the rippling waters of the Straits, trailing droplets of water which sparkled in the light. The steel hawsers of the yachts snapped and keened in the sharp wind which came from nowhere. Martin loved the cormorants. She loved the Monkey Puzzle.

There was a time when people thought that she and Martin were an "item", and they used to laugh out loud together. Their little secret. Not that, in the old days, she wouldn't have liked it to be true but that was never going to happen. Martin wasn't interested in women – not in that way anyway.

One summer evening when they were watching the world go by, Martin turned to her and said, "If I had to have a woman, it would be you." He examined his manicured fingernails as if they were precious gold.

June didn't know how to answer him. She glanced sideways. There was a sadness in the drooping of his head, the hopelessness of his eyes.

"I don't think it would work out for us," June said trying to make light of the situation. "You could never stand my messiness and I can't cook either."

Martin laughed and it broke the spell.

"Too right there," he said. "I'd kill you after five minutes. Remember when you crumpled my cushions? It took me days to get them back into shape." He paused. "Look over there." He pointed to where a flock of cormorants were swirling and tracking across the rippling waves. "I bet they don't worry about cushions."

The moment had passed, and together they rose from the bench and began to walk back to the town as the shadows fell, and the wind turned chilly. They strolled in silence each deep in their own thoughts.

June remembered when they were teenagers. Always together, part of the gang, laughing, leaping into the sea from the pier. Martin was the best-looking boy in their crowd. All the girls fancied him and so did June. He was lithe and strong, his black hair curling into the nape of his neck and his bright blue eyes flashing. He was dare-devil, but always treated the girls in a good way, not like the other boys who could be crude and clumsy. That was his attraction she supposed – along with his sunburned muscular torso and long legs. She was the quiet one, the timid girl who held back when the other girls pushed forward. She knew that she was laughed at. Martin had begun to seek her company when the precociousness of the other girls got too much for him. After a while, it was presumed that they were together, and the girls stopped bothering Martin. June enjoyed the kudos of being "Martin's girl", even though their relationship never went further than holding hands. Then he went away to university and June became an object of pity.

"Do you hear from him?" said Anthea. A gang of girls

had surrounded June in the street. June shook her head and hurried along, closely followed by a determined Anthea.

"Oh, that's such a shame. Never mind there are many more fish in the sea."

She clenched her fists and glared at Anthea. She didn't want "many more fish", she wanted Martin. Anthea flashed a false sympathetic smile and re-joined her group of friends.

"I'm not surprised she hasn't heard from him. Look at her clothes, came off a scarecrow I shouldn't wonder. What would Martin ever see in her?" said Anthea.

The gaggle of girls passed down the road giggling and whispering. June shuffled her way down an alley to avoid their gazes.

"I'll show them," she shouted at a basking cat. "I'll go and see him. That'll shut them up." The cat blinked a lazy eyelid and flicked its tail.

Once home, June scrabbled in her drawer to find Martin's address. She found it under an old pair of socks. They had written to each other once or twice, but the correspondence had faltered. She found a postcard in the desk and addressed it. Turning it over she sat for agonising minutes trying to decide how she should word it. At last, she made up her mind.

Coming to Liverpool to go shopping. Wouldn't it be lovely to meet for coffee or lunch or dinner or even a walk by the docks? It's been so long. She signed it *yours June.* She flapped it about in the air to dry the ink. June always used a fountain pen.

The following Saturday, June made her way to the railway station and boarded the train hoping to look more confident than she felt. She pulled her old green coat around her and polished her only pair of court shoes by rubbing them against the opposite leg. She combed her brown hair with

182

her fingers. When the train pulled in Martin was waiting on the platform. He looked different. His hair was slightly longer, his clothes more flamboyant, but he was now living in the city and was bound to be more fashionable. He had a friend with him, an older man, dressed in elegant cream chinos and a lilac shirt. The man wore his fair hair a little too long. She judged him to be around thirty-five. It would be nice to meet Martin's friends, although she would feel a little out of her depth in intellectual company.

"June," Martin said, rushing forward and taking her hands in his. "It's lovely to see you, let's go and get lunch and catch up. I've so much to tell you. This is Justin, my partner." He indicated the man who moved forward to greet her.

"Lovely to meet you too, June," said Justin. "Martin talks about you so much. I can't wait to hear about his past." Justin laughed and took hold of Martin's arm.

"Nice to meet you Justin." June swallowed hard. She watched as the men strolled along together, their easy familiarity striking deep within her. That used to be her and Martin. She was the odd one out again. She struggled to keep up with them in the unaccustomed shoes.

"We're here," said Martin, turning to look for her as he pushed open the plate glass door of an Italian restaurant. "I booked us a table for lunch. I thought you'd like this place."

June entered the restaurant. The noise hit her as soon as she walked in, Saturday people laughing, shouting, having fun. She wanted to run but stopped herself; she couldn't let him think she was upset. After all, they had never been more than friends.

"Ah, good afternoon Martin," said the maître d'. "Your usual table? I see you have another friend with you today. Welcome, Madam." He gave June a slight nod and moved expertly through the thronging crowd to lead them to a

183

corner table. It was obvious to June that Martin was well known here and that made her more uncomfortable. She had never been in a restaurant as nice as this one before.

Once seated and the food ordered, Martin turned to June who was fidgeting with the edge of the tablecloth.

"It's a long time since I saw you. What really brought you to Liverpool, although I can see you really need to do some shopping?" He eyed her old green coat and scuffed court shoes and raised his eyebrows. She should have laughed, accepted his comment like she would have done before. But something had changed.

She felt her eyelashes begin to dampen; she couldn't let him see her cry. She jumped up from the table throwing her napkin down.

"What's happened to you Martin?" she cried, "I thought we were friends."

"Sit down, June, don't make a fuss," he answered, trying to pull her back down into her seat. "I'm sorry."

"Are you?" she replied. "Or are you showing off in front of Justin? Sorry I can't stay."

She was being oversensitive and making a fool of herself, but she didn't care. She pushed her way past the maître d' who was bringing their drinks.

Once outside on the street, she steadied her trembling legs. Then she felt angry. This was not her Martin. How dare he? After all those years she had protected him, befriended him, gave him her life. If she wasn't good enough for him now, well she didn't want him either. She and Martin didn't contact each other again. The years passed.

One afternoon in late May, she was walking to the shops when she heard a shout behind her.

"June? Is that you June?" A grey-haired man came limping up to her, his cane tapping on the pavement.

184

She turned, squinting her eyes against the sunlight. She recognised Martin although he seemed shrunken, and his face was lined. She noticed he was wearing an old, battered overcoat and his trousers were creased. His grey hair was thinning on top and his blue eyes watered. She hurried on, not wishing to engage with him again, but he caught her up.

"June, it's me, Martin," he called. "Please stop."

Unsure, she waited. When he halted beside her, he was out of breath and had to lean on his stick for support.

"Hello Martin, where's Justin? I'm surprised you're on your own."

"Touché, June," he whispered, now leaning on the wall. "We broke up many years ago. He found someone better." His laugh was brittle as he caught his breath. "I wrote to you to apologise, you know."

"Well, I never got a letter." She wasn't sure whether to believe him or not.

"Let's go get a coffee and talk," he said, taking her arm. She shook free of his grasp but walked beside him.

Inside the café, he paid for the coffees and led the way to a window table.

"I'm sorry for being such a brat June, it was unforgiveable."

"Yes, it was," she replied, stirring her coffee vigorously although she didn't take sugar. She didn't elaborate on the hurt she had felt, and he didn't ask. He didn't elaborate on his illness, and she did not probe. He told her he had bought a house in the town.

"What made you come back?" she asked. "And where have you been all these years?"

"Oh, here and there. You know how it is," he replied.

"No, I don't know how it is," she retorted, shredding her napkin. "Tell me."

"You don't want to know," he said. She saw a darkness creep across his eyes.

They sat in silence for a few minutes before Martin spoke again.

"I can't tell you," he said, reaching out for her hand. This time she did not avoid his touch. "I hope we can be friends again."

She squeezed his bony fingers in response.

They arranged to meet each day come rain or shine on a special bench by the seashore. They laughed and cried, watched the cormorants, and derided the public, then one day Martin did not turn up. June waited for an hour on that solitary bench by the Monkey Puzzle tree. She was worried and she played many different scenarios in her mind as she hurried along. Had Justin returned?

When she reached his home, there was an ambulance parked outside. The house door was ajar. She pushed it gently and walked inside. There were strangers there, uniforms. No one noticed her presence, as a stretcher was brought downstairs. A tuft of Martin's grey hair peeped from under the blue hospital blanket he was swaddled in. His eyes were closed. She stretched out a hand to touch him, but she was jostled out of the way.

"Are you family?" asked the man in uniform.

"No," she replied, moving aside, "just a friend, his best friend. His lifelong best friend."

In late September, she noticed the Monkey Puzzle had grown; it was now up to the second-floor window of the house. She pulled her paisley scarf, Martin's favourite, close around her neck against the chill as she watched the cormorants skimming the water, their bright plumage sleek with sea water.

"There they go Martin, see how beautiful they are."

186

About the author

Liz has been writing short stories and poetry for twenty years and is currently completing a historical novel. With a PhD in Medieval Studies, she has used this background to enrich her writing. She has short stories published with CaféLit, Bridge House and www.potatosoupjournal.com. Two of her poems were published in *Coed* an anthology supporting the campaign to save Penrhos Nature Reserve on Anglesey and her poem was accepted for the *Plantation for Poems* project organised by Bideford Library in 2020. She lives in North Yorkshire.

The Green-Eyed Angel

Linda Flynn

"Jealousy can open the blood, it can make black roses." **Sylvia Plath**

"Appearing better than others is always dangerous, but most dangerous of all is to appear to have no faults or weaknesses. Envy creates silent enemies." **Robert Greene**

Detective Digby used swift, smooth movements to ease her wheelchair in front of the patio doors, as she pretended to observe the snowy scene outside. She liked to watch people when they didn't know she was looking. The crackling fire and sparkling lights threw back the reflection of the drawing room; a perfect setting for the Christmas festivities. The room was dominated by a Norwegian spruce draped with fairy lights, sweetly scented with slices of dried orange, cinnamon and cloves and topped by a golden-haired angel. A heavy silence fell, punctuated by the ticking of the clock, the hissing flames and the spitting logs.

Three women in their early thirties sat rigidly in their chairs, their angular bodies twisted away from each other. *Three frenemies in front of a fire. And it should have been four.*

Even when Constable Tom Gawk knocked his shins into a coffee table, she continued to face forward. She watched him rush into the kitchen for a cloth to mop up a spilt whiskey. Normally she wouldn't make a house call so early on for a missing person, especially on Christmas Eve, but she learned long ago to listen to the instinct that was tugging her, the uncanny sense of dread.

188

Digby spun her chair around and smiled, keen to justify her silence. "Someone's been busy outside." She threw back her arm, "Is that a snow angel? It's rather beautiful. Look at the delicately feathered wings and folds in the gown."

"Yes." Sarah nodded, pushing back her blonde highlighted hair. "It was there when we arrived. It's a snow sculpture."

Tom emerged from the doorway. "It's been over twenty-four hours now since Angelica Drape's disappearance. Please would all of you try to get hold of her friends, ring around anyone she might visit and try social media. We'll carry out some checks in the area. I've left our contact details in the kitchen. Please call if you hear anything."

All night Digby listened to the wind moaning in the eaves, as a cold draft swept under her bedroom door. Dreams of distorted snowflakes swirled around her head, morphing from symmetrical crystalline shapes to jagged icicle daggers.

She woke abruptly to the shriek of her phone. "Tom…" She rubbed her eyes. "It is four o'clock on Christmas morning. Unless you're Santa Claus, go back to bed."

"I've got a sack full of presents for you; well actually it's Angelica's holdall. It was found near the railway cutting, about a mile before the station and close to the women's rental property."

As the car scrunched up the driveway in the hazy dawn, Digby noticed a curtain twitch. She switched off the ignition and faced Tom. "When you went into the kitchen, did you notice if the broom was wet?"

Tom nodded, "Yes, it was standing in a pool of water, presumably from clearing the front porch."

A light pattering of rain fell, thawing the snow outside,

189

but the atmosphere inside remained icy. Digby swivelled her chair around the room, watching the women's pale faces as they sat hunched in their dressing gowns. "I'm sorry to disturb you so early on Christmas morning, but new information has come to light and so I would like to ask you all a few questions."

She swung around as Tom cried out, "The snow angel!"

Around its face gold tufts stuck out, almost like a halo. The rain fell faster, leaving unrelenting trails against the window. Digby's hands flew up, as an alabaster face emerged. Blurry reflections of horror were thrown back in the glass. Somewhere in the room she heard a whimper, as pale blue clothing seeped through the snow, draped in slippery folds. Right in the centre bloomed a scarlet blotch, like a rose.

Digby rubbed the sides of her head. "We will have to detain you all with a police officer, while we investigate this crime further and allow our dogs to search the house and grounds. No-one must leave. We will return later in the afternoon to conduct interviews."

"Great Christmas this is turning out to be!" moaned Tom as he slammed the car door. "No turkey, no presents, not even a whiff of alcohol." He noticed Digby's air of abstraction. "Are we any further forward?"

"Not really. There's a positive identification that the victim is Angelica Drape and the holdall belongs to her. Forensics said that the murder was conducted with a sharp, cone-shaped object. The police teams and dogs have swept through the house and grounds, but found little conclusive evidence. Without the murder weapon…"

"Surely it can't be far away? It has to be one of those three women, supposedly a friend. But how do you think they did it?"

"Well, let me see," pondered Digby. "If I decided to murder you, I would place a silver coin in the Christmas pudding and wait for you to swallow it."

Tom glanced sideways and Digby smiled, "Don't worry, I won't kill you while you're useful. Actually, there's something I'd like you to do for me."

Tom groaned.

Already the drawing room was filling with darkness, relieved by the pinpricks of fairy lights. Digby abandoned any attempts at false jollity. "Good evening, ladies. I will be conducting interviews in the adjoining study and while these take place, no-one must leave the room. I will begin with Chloe."

Tom rushed forward to open the door, but his ankle snagged against the tree, which fell to the floor in a tinkling crash. There was a gasp, as the lights flickered for a moment and then collapsed the room into darkness.

Digby sighed. "Sarah, please would you light the candles, until Tom has managed to fix the fuse."

Chloe fumbled for a chair, with the candle shaking in her hand, casting distorted shadows on the wall. She stared at the floor as her cropped blonde hair accentuated her clenched jaw.

A brief silence elapsed, before Digby asked, "So, I'm curious, what was Angelica like? Did you know her well?"

Chloe's head shot up. "Not as well as Freia. They were inseparable at primary school, until a bit of rivalry set in. They even looked a bit alike in those days, with their auburn hair and green eyes. Angelica was one of those people who seemed to drift swan-like through life, from the catwalk to the stage." Digby nodded, but thought that under the surface there would have been a lot of paddling.

Digby leaned forward. "I know this has been a terrible shock for you, but if you don't mind me saying so, you've been very quiet, even before the murder came to light. You don't seem very happy to be here... None of you do really."

Chloe hunched into her chair, with her arms tucked around her knees. "Well no, it's not exactly my usual kind of Christmas."

"What do you mean by that?"

Chloe's eyes glinted. "I mean that this time last year I was setting up home with my fiancé."

"What happened?"

"Another woman happened, that's what!"

"Anyone you know?"

Chloe gave an angry laugh, "Yeah, you could say that."

"And he left you?"

"No." Chloe shook her head so that her jagged Christmas tree earrings refracted in the candle light. "But it was too late by then, the damage was done. I don't believe in second chances. He said it was just a fling, that he'd been besotted by her attention, that he'd made a mistake. I said too right he'd made a mistake and that I never want to see him again!"

Digby's brow creased. "You couldn't forgive and forget?"

Chloe stared directly ahead. "No."

"Hello, Freia." Digby smiled as she led a wispy woman into the study. Her burnished hair shone in the candlelight, but it accentuated the hollows under her eyes.

Digby noticed the whiteness of her knuckles, as she clenched her barrel bag. She heard a clinking sound. "What are you keeping in your bag?"

"Oh, skewers." She passed it over to Digby's outstretched hand, with flushed cheeks. "Sarah's a bit bossy and she assigned us all roles. Mine was to cook the turkey, and I doubted that a rental house would provide any skewers to check it. Then after the murder, there was no way that I was going to leave these around."

Digby placed them in a clear plastic bag as she spoke, "I gather that you and Angelica go way back. I'm trying to build up a bit of a picture of her in my head. What was she like in school?"

Freia slipped her free hand through her coppery curls. "Oh, you know, little miss popular, copied by the girls, adored by the boys, even the teachers admired her intelligence. She seemed to shine at everything she turned her hand to."

Digby reflected that people like to dislike perfection. She gave a sympathetic nod, "That must have been quite irritating at times."

"Oh, it was! Don't get me wrong, she was a nice person and all the rest of it. It's just that everything came too easily to her: star of the school play, good at sports, top exam results. And the worst of it was that she didn't seem to notice how lucky she was, she just expected it all to fall into her lap – including the boys – and believe me they did!"

"I see from the phone records that you made the most calls to Angelica's mobile. Why was that?"

Freia frowned. "I was worried about her. She was supposed to have been one of the first to arrive."

"Before you?"

"Yes."

"But you caught the 9.32 train. CCTV places you both climbing into the same carriage from Rickmansworth Station. Which means that you would have arrived together."

Freia shifted in her seat. "Well, not exactly."

"Why?"

"I realise now that this doesn't look good. I'd said I would travel with her for company on the train, but then we had a blazing row. I got so irritated with her that I climbed out a stop earlier and slammed the door. I needed to calm down."

"What was the argument about?"

193

"Oh, I don't know, something of nothing. Angelica disapproved of my new partner and kept going on and on, even when I told her that I'm not seeing him anymore. She could be a bit self-righteous at times."

"And that made you angry? It seems like a bit of a dramatic reaction."

"Maybe, but I also didn't want to be there when Sarah asked Angelica a favour. Sarah was hoping that Angelica would pull a few strings for her at the Playhouse Theatre, where she's acting, see if she could get her some work in props and scenery. It would put Angelica in an awkward situation and I know she wouldn't have been happy. It's also a bit humiliating for Sarah, especially as she's got a few years of experience under her belt, but she's been a bit down on her luck lately."

"So did you see Angelica after you got off the train?"

"No and that's why I was so concerned when she hadn't turned up before me."

"Thank you, Freia. Please would you send Sarah in?

"Do take a seat, Sarah," said Digby looking up. She noted that Sarah looked efficient, with a notepad on her lap and a pencil tucked behind her ear. "According to my notes, the booking was made in your name."

Sarah smiled. "That's right. We all found ourselves at a loose end this Christmas, so instead of moping on our own, I thought it'd be entertaining if we all got together."

"And you were the first to arrive?"

"No, that'd be Chloe. She was already parked in the driveway when I arrived – she's always early. Once I unlocked the door, she put her bag in the best, front-facing bedroom, then went out to collect some of the groceries I'd ordered."

Digby nodded. "And Angelica was supposed to arrive early to help you decorate the house and tree? Surely you could have done that alone?"

194

"Yes, of course, I did in the end. But I thought it'd be more fun, as well as easier to bring the tree in from outside. And no-one can do things quite as well as Angelica."

"I see. So, what was she like?"

"Oh, you know, always the one to shine. When Angelica was in the room the rest of us might as well be invisible."

Digby smiled. "Did it go to her head a bit?"

Sarah shrugged, but the flickering candle threw shade in the downward crevices of her mouth. "No, she took it in her stride. Don't think she even noticed."

Digby leaned forward and lowered her voice. "I get the impression that she was rather irresistible to men. Is that why Chloe's fiancé had an affair with her?"

Sarah snorted. "That wasn't Angelica, it was Freia."

"Freia?"

"Yes. I knew, but kept quiet about it. Freia was happy to let Angelica take the blame. There's not been much love lost between those two – they've always been rivals."

"I see. That would have made for an uncomfortable gathering."

"I suppose so. I was hoping we'd be able to heal the rift. We've known each other for so many years."

"Thank you, Sarah. Let's go and join the others."

Digby slid her chair into the centre of the darkened room, lit only by three candles. "This was a crime executed in jealousy and bitterness, hidden behind a beautiful snow angel. The murderer theatrically placed Angelica's corpse where it would be the centre of attention in death, just as she had been all her life.

"This led me to think that the culprit would place the murder weapon somewhere conspicuous too, without us even realising it. Please turn the fuse switch back on, Tom."

Everyone blinked in the brightness. "We were staring at it all the time." She held up a clear plastic bag containing

195

the spike of the Christmas tree holder. "I am sure forensics will confirm that this is the murder weapon.

"We were all dazzled by the sparkling lights and the golden angel on top, but you Sarah, your eyes kept travelling to the bottom of the tree. This murder wasn't premeditated; you grabbed the first implement that came to hand, when Angelica hesitated to recommend you for a job backstage. Your skill at creating props is demonstrated by the craftsmanship shown in the snow sculpture."

The others turned to stare at Sarah, who uncoiled herself from her chair and spat, "Like the sugary cake decoration, Angelica was so sickly sweet!"

Digby continued, "And really, who would even think of using the spike of a Christmas tree holder as a murder weapon?

"You knew that we would search the house with dogs, so the pine needles, orange, cloves and cinnamon would help to disguise the scent of blood."

"The dramatic, theatrical way you chose to slowly reveal the body ended up revealing your crime."

As Tom led Sarah away, Digby decided that she would raise a glass to a Christmas night that she too would spend in silence and solitude.

About the author

Linda Flynn has had books published for children and teenagers, six with the Heinemann Fiction Project, as well as over twenty short stories, mainly written for adults. In addition, she has written for a number of newspapers and magazines, including theatre reviews. Linda was a winner in the Globe Soup Historical category around the theme, *Knowledge is Power* in December 2021 with Shadow Play. Her collection of short stories, *I Knew It In The Bath* was released in September 2022 with Bridge House. Two children's books have recently been published with Chapeltown Books: *A Most Amazing Zoo* and *Santa's Supersonic Sleigh*. She can be found at: www.lindaflynn.com

In With the New

Jo Fino

This is my seventh attic. Although it's really a loft, a conversion I heard Pea say, and it smells of oak and cedar and rosemary and sage. I finally have large picture windows, and every day I have changing views. I have seen trees in variegated hues, the glint of myriad blues from the lake, and the sun peeking its head over the mountain in the early morning. By mid-day in summer my loft was swathed with sunlight. In the inkiness of the night, stars forever slyly winking at me, and the moon grinning shyly at owls hooting on high, as the ground below rustles with the bustle of industrious rodents.

Pea joins me most mornings, each familiar creak heralding her, as she climbs the stairs, her spicy perfume and intensity of her caffeine fix bringing her closer to me. After years of predominantly quiet reflection, I was unsure how I would cope with prolonged, rather than specific and sporadic exposure to Pea's company. I am so used, you see, to my own space and the time I have to consider Pea and Lincoln's life. I admit in the beginning I found her constant tap tap tapping away on the keyboard, and the lingering smell of coffee a little irksome. But I learnt to filter it out and tune in to the spattering of bird chatter, the guarded whisperings of the leaves in the wind, the hints of lavender and jasmine in the air, and the stealthy backslap of the lake. Pea rarely speaks when she works, and certainly not to me; although there is the odd muttering or swear word. I actually miss hearing her deep tones, but I don't miss the shouting. It's not what I'm generally disposed towards, and last time when there was a lot of it, I remember Pea pushing past me so that I thought I might fall over. It didn't seem too long after that when everything was piled into a huge van and we came here.

"More coffee Pea?" Lincoln's tone has been gentler since we moved.

"Yes please darling." Pea, in turn always sounds appreciative now. Something has altered then, between them. From their exchanges when he brings the coffee I have learnt that Lincoln has a new routine too. He no longer goes away on long trips, but works in another part of the house which Pea calls his "Dungeon", Lincoln in turn calling her space "The Heights". They have had visitors, but no one I would care for. Sometimes if Pea left the window open in the loft, I heard them: the pop of a cork, the silvery clink of crystal, the strains of Pea's Latin American vibes, and the rolling hum of voices peppered with chinks of laughter. In the summer, charcoal, wood smoke and charring meat drifted upwards in the late evening breeze, but now we're deep into winter, the house is silent again, and Pea works in thick jumpers and socks. The sun very rarely shows its face; much less its comfy embrace, and sometimes I wonder why she doesn't turn the heater on. But I don't really mind. Cold or hot, it's all the same to me, and I think it keeps Pea sharp. "On her game" is a phrase I've heard her use in the past.

This morning I noticed she's brought her phone up with her. She seems distracted and each time it buzzes she picks it up, frowns, sighs, swipes sideways, and puts it down carefully. There's been no tap tapping on her computer for a while and she's got up and walked to the window several times.

"Any news yet?" Lincoln surprises me. I'm so focussed on Pea I didn't hear him arrive. He's brought two coffee cups and as he places Pea's on her desk he trails his hand over the back of hers. She looks up, shakes her head and

198

smiles at him. But her eyes are dim, the smile a token stretching of her lips, showing gratitude, while the furrows on her forehead scream weeks of worry and sorrow. Why have I not noticed this before? Too busy taking in new experiences for myself, I suppose, but I shouldn't lose sight of my family.

Lincoln has perched on the low settee in the corner now and I can't really see his face, but I hear him slurp his coffee through the silence that has settled between them. Pea's phone buzzes again and as she picks it up I hear her suck in a breath and puff it out, as if she's about to do something really momentous. Then she smiles. A proper smile this time. "It's him, Linc. It's Malachi. He's coming home. Oh my God Linc, oh my God." And then she scoots across the oak floor and she's in Lincoln's arms and she's crying. Which is quite surprising, as I haven't seen such a public display of affection between them for some time.

So Malachi is coming here, to the new house. Therefore I presume it must be nearly time for me to move. I have, I admit, missed the tinny thrashing of his rock music, the low thrum of his bass guitar, the patter of his basketball and faint waft of weed when Pea and Lincoln are safely out of the house. Malachi has come and gone over the last few years, living his own life now he's all grown up, but he always comes back, eventually. He was the same when he was a little boy even, losing track of time, and then as a teenager, seeming to have no concept of it any more. I remember hearing Pea reminding him how she would leave frantic messages on multiple numbers, before jumping in her convertible to go looking for him, and how surprised Malachi would always be when she found him. Lincoln on the other hand would shake his head, ruffle Malachi's hair and say, "Always your mama's boy, Mal, and you always will be." And Malachi would pretend to shrug his dad off, but he would have that big happy grin on

199

his face as he popped open another beer. I wonder where he's been this time though? Pea's reaction to the news seems over the top to me, as if something has happened to keep Malachi away. I have obviously missed this. I filter through fragments of memory, but as always there are gaps, and I begin to wonder if I spent longer in the previous house than it actually seemed.

"So when is he coming?" Lincoln has managed to prise Pea off and she's wiping her eyes.

"He said he's managed to get a flight back a week on Friday. So all being well late on the Saturday night. Oh Linc, we need to start getting things ready, right away!" Pea jumps up and knocks the remnants of Lincoln's coffee over, but she doesn't even seem to notice. She's waving her hands around and pacing. "I think we should do things differently this time. Starting with the smudging, I want this to be a new start, everything needs to be fresh and organic and… new, and positive, full of positive energy."

I see her eyes sweep the room, taking me in briefly and I'm not entirely sure I like the sound of this; I'm not a great fan of change. But Lincoln is speaking again and I need to concentrate.

"And Jade? What about Jade, Pea? Is she coming too?"

Pea stops pacing. "No. I don't know; he doesn't know."

"No, Malachi doesn't know, or no, she's not coming? What did he say, Perpetua, what did he say?" Lincoln only ever uses Pea's full name when he's angry, irritated by her, or both.

"He didn't say." Pea turns away from Lincoln and frowns. It's the one I've seen over the years, where she's considering her words carefully. "He didn't say anything about her on the message."

From my corner I watch her face and I think she's lying to him.

"And – you didn't ask?" Lincoln stands up now too and he puts his hands on Pea's shoulders and swings her round to face him. "Why Pea? Why?"

It was Christmas time when I heard Lincoln say those same words to Pea. I think it was last Christmas? He just sounded so sad, and he sat and watched as Pea wept big silent heaving sobs, shuddering and rocking back and forward. I had never seen her like that before. Sure they sometimes rowed around me, but it always seemed light hearted bickering in the main. When they were little the children were oblivious, playing together with their new toys, or with invited family guests. Soon after, Pea and Lincoln would put it to one side, open a bottle of champagne, or grab a beer, and later they would all play games or watch a movie. As Malachi and Jade got older they would bring their friends and then partners around. But not last time, last Christmas. It was strange. Malachi wasn't there at all and Jade left straight after the huge row with Pea.

I had heard Jade and Pea exchange views before. But Pea seemed angry, in that dangerously low voice; lips stitched together type of way. She was reading from her phone screen.

Content is King but who is its Queen?
Affectionately known as Pea to her close friends, reverently referred to as PVD by her growing and fanatical tribe, just who is Perpetua Vers (silent "s") Dant?
This self-styled Content Curator has amassed her wealth off the back of other people's hard work and research, and now has the audacity to appropriate the climate change agenda for her own ends.
Her latest content rich site describes her as an

Eco ninja, conservationista, enviro sista, naturista.
All very "down with the woke brigade". Yet she has
no credible claim to any activity that warrants such
monikers, and her own daughter, Jade, had this to
say: "She's a fake, her name is totally phoney, and
she's brainwashed her followers into believing
everything she lays down on her social media. She
doesn't even recycle properly FFS!"
The rumour is that all of PVD's channels are
actually written and run by Lincoln green. Who is
also alleged to be PVD's reclusive husband.
OR are they one and the same person?

I didn't hear much of the rest of it. Jade said it was a
total misquote and flounced out of the room, Pea followed
and the row clearly escalated from there. The upshot after
Jade left was a long conversation out of my ear shot
between Pea and Lincoln, once she calmed down. The next
morning I was despatched back to the attic, feeling
decidedly left out and short changed.

It's always winter, the last few times Malachi and Jade
have been around the house. I used to hear them all year,
singing, shouting, crying, clattering up the stairs with a
gang of friends, and sometimes disturbing me. But I didn't
mind that because it made me feel safe to know they were
there, and I would soon be needed. And I waited patiently
for my time to shine with them.

In my loft I can see that there are more changes in the
air and the light and the temperature than I ever knew. Days
last longer, nights are shorter and time slowly begins to
make more sense to me now.

Lincoln is talking again. "You know how much I've
missed her Pea, and you swore to me you were going to
make it right."

"And I will Linc. I promise you I will. Just give it a little more time. I've missed her too."

"That's it though Pea. I don't know how much more time I can give it. I should have gone after her myself. What were we thinking sending Malachi?" Lincoln sits down on the settee again and I see how drained he looks. It's almost as if I am seeing both of them more clearly as my days in the loft have spun out.

"You know you couldn't go Linc. You're still not well enough." Pea took his hand. "Please just trust me and Mal. We will get her back."

Lincoln looks up at Pea and I see how he clutches her hand tighter. "In time for Christmas? Do you promise Pea?"

Pea nods, and glances over at me and this time I believe her face, and I feel light and giddy and suddenly excited.

It's a week later and Pea hasn't stopped as far as I can tell. She's hardly spent any time in the loft since she collected her "smudging" materials: the abalone shells and sticks she had made from a mixture of herbs including sage, rosemary, and cedar leaves. I believe from what I can hear down below that an intense cleaning and re organisation of rooms is underway. I'm curious to see how it will all look, and find my space in the unfolding tableau she is creating. She intends to burn the herbs in the abalone shells in rooms in the house, in order to cleanse the spaces and invite in positive energy. Going by previous form, she will enact the final cleansing of the family lounge on Christmas Eve, as I have seen her do before. It was one Christmas, I forget which, when Jade gifted her mum the shells and original herb sticks, along with a very specific explanation of how Pea should be aware of the dangers of cultural misappropriation. Jade was also very clear, that Pea should be careful how she shared information about it on her social media. I know there was a lot of discussion around the origins and rituals of smudging, but it was too much for me with everything else that was going on that day. It did also start a tradition of Lincoln gifting Pea exquisitely fashioned and spiritually significant abalone jewellery, which I'm sure was also Jade's idea.

Jade was a serious, precise, yet sweet child, gentle and thoughtful in her ways, whereas Malachi was cheeky, a little rough but totally adorable. Born with an old soul, there was a timelessness about Jade and I warmed to her. I would watch how her eyes constantly sought out her mama, looking for approbation and encouragement, even that last Christmas. I honestly don't know the full extent of the row between Jade and Pea, only that it was bad for everyone in the end, and I can't be entirely sure how Pea feels about Jade right now. But I do know she loves her with all the fierceness and pride a mother can possess, for I have seen it in her face when she thought no one was watching. No one that is, but I.

So now I wait patiently for Pea and Lincoln to fetch me. I know preparations are underway; there have been familiar smells of baking, tyres crunching on gravel, doorbells ringing. Carefully packed boxes have been long since removed from the storage cupboard in the loft and replaced with festively wrapped packages. The exquisite blend of Pea's smudging sticks linger in the air below, and delicate fronds of frost lace the glass panes of the loft. I wait for them to come for me, as I watch each dark sky leak into a milk pale morning, the sun a gentle gleam like a half closed cats eye. I listen for the creak of the stair, long for the lingering hot spice of Pea's scent, and I miss her tap tap tapping. Of Lincoln, I hear nothing, for he has no need to bring me coffee, and I begin to wonder about the illness Pea mentioned. The storage cupboard is empty of plain boxes, save one that stands alone now amongst the red and the gold packages, plastered with Merry Christmas and Ho, Ho, Ho's. It's my box.

Another morning comes and I'm trying to work out how long it will be now. But I don't know how many days there are, and Pea still hasn't been to the loft to collect my box. Then I hear it: the creak of the stair. I smell coffee dark and insidious, snaking through the spindles. Lincoln carries a small bag in one hand, and his coffee cup in the other. He pauses at the top of the stairs, looks over to the open storage cupboard, and throws me a glance. Now, it must be now, surely? But he looks away, and sits down at Pea's desk where he proceeds to wrap some small parcels, more jewellery for her I presume. He puts them all back in the bag, sips from his coffee cup and stares at nothing. Then he opens Pea's desk drawer, takes out her abandoned laptop and turns it on. He taps swiftly and lightly, until it seems he finds what he's looking for, because he swears under his breath and reaches for the coffee cup again. But now I see the cup wobble, his hand trembling as he reads. Lincoln closes his eyes, as if he is making up his mind about something and when he opens them I see they are brimming with unshed tears. I have seen enough of them over the years, I should know. Then he quickly closes down the laptop, puts it back and picks up the bag and cup. At the top of the stairs he pauses and he looks straight at me, then he walks over and he touches me, he trails his hand along me like he did with Pea's hand all those days ago, and he reaches down and places the bag behind me and he whispers, *"In with the new?"* In a second he is gone, his steps light on the wooden stairs in his house slippers.

And I am alone. And I wait.

Two more days have passed, the morning frost is thickening on the outside of the glass, and I feel hopeless. This loft that has given me new life, that I have learned to love, feels now like a prison. I am sectioned off from the heart of the home, at the most critical time and I strain to hear

205

what goes on below. Pea is scurrying everywhere now like a tiny squirrel, her flip flops pattering on the wooden floors, and the aromas of cooking and cleaning and her herbs waft up the stairs through the door left open by Lincoln. I hear her shouting instructions to him (so he is still here then), to someone she has brought in to help, and down the phone to anyone, and no one in particular. It seems to me strange, all this activity for Malachi. Not that I'm not glad he's coming home, of course I am. But I begin to think Pea has invited a whole houseful of distant relatives, dredged up from Facebook, or worse, his old school and college friends. A sure fire car crash of a day, going by past experiences, and guaranteed to upset Lincoln, who is hoping Pea will make good her promise and bring Jade home. Nothing and no one else will do it for Lincoln, not even Malachi.

The light has faded to chalk grey before I even noticed, and birds perch like sentries cast in stone on the leafless spines of the huge tree opposite the loft. They watch and wait as the sky darkens and all I can do is stare them out, and wait. I will not give up hope that the children (for so they will always be to me) will both return. Reinforcements are swooping onto the tree now, but then a rogue fly past spooks them, and through the resultant squawking I hear a car engine down below, doors clunking shut. Gravel crunches underfoot and there is shouting, and a faint high pitched wail which carries through the flung wide open front door, and into the bowels of the house. Voices now are in the hall way, floating up the stairs to me. I hear Pea and then Lincoln, and a man's voice I don't know. And there it is; it's Malachi and I guess he must have brought a friend. Then I hear a small cry, and a voice: that familiar silvery lilt now edged with soothing.

Jade is home. She has brought a baby.

I listen long into the darkness of the night as they eat

206

and talk, and wine is poured and glasses toast, and doors open and close and laughter is constant.

And I am happy for them. For the new life, the new start.

I know the tree in the family lounge will be wonderful and fragrant and fresh, its real scent permeating the air as it mingles with the lavender Pea burns on the open fire. It will be tastefully hung with new decorations, in the latest shades, for my box still sits in the cupboard. Its pearly lights will glow and pick up the shades of the abalone shells Pea so loves. They will all compliment Pea on her efforts and they will instagram happy family photos by it. Tonight Lincoln will visit the loft, to collect all the presents from the cupboard and Pea will artfully arrange them under the tree. In the morning they will all gather around, while Lincoln makes one last trip to me, to retrieve his bag of gifts for Pea.

But when the "real" tree begins to dry and bow and shed its needles, no matter what they do, Jade will already be thinking how the baby will be mobile next year. And she will remember me, carefully stored away in the loft, and the box of treasured childhood decorations she secretly missed this Christmas, and she will eventually come for me.

And I will patiently wait as I have done, for all these years.

About the author
Jo Fino says she is a dreamer, an optimist, a worrier too. She started writing again to deal with a stressful situation and gradually rediscovered her passion. She now chairs a successful North Wales Writing Group. She has been published on the *CaféLit* site and in *The Best of CaféLit 3*. She was also shortlisted by Honno in their call for ghost stories and her short story *Cruel Summer* won the Writers' Forum monthly competition and was published in issue 146.

Index of Authors

Like to Read More Work Like This?

Then sign up to our mailing list and download our free collection of short stories, *Magnetism*. Sign up now to receive this free e-book and also to find out about all of our new publications and offers.

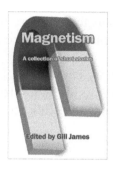

Sign up here:
   http://eepurl.com/gbpdVz

Please Leave a Review

Reviews are so important to writers. Please take the time to review this book. A couple of lines is fine.

Reviews help the book to become more visible to buyers. Retailers will promote books with multiple reviews.

This in turn helps us to sell more books... And then we can afford to publish more books like this one.

Leaving a review is very easy.

Go to https://bit.ly/3X8KAvf, scroll down the left-hand side of the Amazon page and click on the "Write a customer review" button.

Other Publications by Bridge House

Resolutions

edited by Debz Hobbs-Wyatt and Gill James

Resolve is high. Determination rules OK. Human spirit excels.

This is a collection of challenging and thought-provoking stories. All stories need a resolution and these provide ones that will astound and delight you. We looked for story, good writing, interpretation of theme, and professionalism. All of the stories submitted had those elements. Here we offer a variety to cater to our readers' eclectic tastes. Sit back and surrender to the Bridge House magic.

Resolutions is a themed multi-author collection from Bridge House Publishing

"A delightful and amusing collection of stories from some very talented writers. More power to the short story." (*Amazon*)

Order from Amazon:

Paperback: ISBN 978-1-914199-10-3
eBook: ISBN 978-1-914199-11-0

Mulling It Over

edited by Debz Hobbs-Wyatt and Gill James

The Island of Mull, covered in mulls. To mull a drink. An important instrument for making a book. Plenty to mull over here. And plenty to make you think.

As ever, the interpretation has been varied: the Island of Mull, thinking about things, often quite deeply, the odd mulled drink and even something used in making a book - how appropriate again. You will find a variety of styles here and an intriguing mix of voices. There is humour and pathos, some hard-hitting tales and some feel-good accounts. All to be mulled over.

"The Island of Mull is a great concept - we all have had plenty to mull over in 2020. It's a great collection of stories. Very well done!" (*Amazon*)

Order from Amazon:

Paperback: ISBN 978-1-907335-93-8
eBook: ISBN 978-1-907335-94-5

Nativity

edited by Debz Hobbs-Wyatt and Gill James

Many of the stories in this collection take place at or near Christmas time. There are stories of new births, of rebirths, of new beginnings, and there are a couple that deal with the joys and sorrows of the annual Nativity Play.

There are some familiar authors in this volume and also some new writers. We treasure them all.

"A most unexpected collection of stories, focused on new beginnings and rebirth. It's definitely not your traditional nativity theme, but so much more. The stories are so varied, dramatic, melancholic, dark and comedic, there is a story to suit everyone." (*Amazon*)

Order from Amazon:

Paperback: ISBN 978-1-907335-76-1
eBook: ISBN 978-1-907335-77-8

Lightning Source UK Ltd.
Milton Keynes UK
UKHW021817041222
413331UK00012B/301